Nice Girls Don't

Sue Barnard

CROOKED CAT

Discover us online:
www.crookedcatpublishing.com

Join us on facebook:
www.facebook.com/crookedcatpublishing

Tweet a photo of yourself holding
this book to @crookedcatbooks
and something nice will happen.

For R.
Love always.

About the Author

Sue Barnard was born in North Wales but has spent most of her life in and around Manchester. After graduating from Durham University, where she studied French and Italian, Sue got married then had a variety of office jobs before becoming a full-time parent. If she had her way, the phrase "non-working mother" would be banned from the English language.

Since then she has had a series of part-time jobs, including some work as a freelance copywriter. In parallel with this she took several courses in Creative Writing. Her writing achievements include winning the Writing Magazine New Subscribers Poetry Competition for 2013.

Sue has a mind which is sufficiently warped as to be capable of compiling questions for BBC Radio 4's fiendishly difficult *Round Britain Quiz*. This once caused one of her sons to describe her as "professionally weird". The label has stuck.

Sue joined the editorial team Crooked Cat Publishing in 2013. Her first novel, *The Ghostly Father* (a new take on the traditional story of Romeo & Juliet), was officially released on St Valentine's Day 2014. She's still trying to get her head round the fact that people actually bought it, read it and enjoyed it.

When Sue isn't writing, she enjoys travelling, reading, amateur dramatics, walking and gardening (she claims she's had some of her best writing ideas when she's been mowing the lawn). She is also very interested in Family History. Her own background is stranger than fiction; she'd write a book about it if she thought anybody would believe her.

Nice Girls Don't, which is her second novel, is not that book.

Acknowledgements

Once again I am eternally grateful to Laurence & Steph Patterson, of Crooked Cat Publishing, for believing in this story. Thanks too to my fab editor, Christine McPherson – it was a pleasure working with you!

This book would never have happened without the unfailing help, support, encouragement and guidance of my wonderful friend and mentor Sally Quilford (who taught me everything I know about writing romance) and my superb writing buddies Miriam Drori and Gail Richards (who both gave such valuable feedback on the manuscript). To all of you, very many thanks.

Special thanks are again due to my wonderful husband Bob, who patiently tolerates sharing his life and his home with a particularly crazy example of what the great W S Gilbert once described as "that singular anomaly".

Finally, whilst this is a work of fiction (and none of the characters are modelled on real people), I must confess that two of the episodes described in the story are based, at least in part, on actual events. I won't reveal which, but I must say a special thank-you to all the members of my extended family, who showed me that my family tree, like most family trees, is full of nuts!

Sue Barnard
July 2014

Nice Girls Don't

Chapter One

1982

"Emily? Are you up? It's almost twenty-to-ten!"

The hammering on the bedroom door hauled Emily into semi-consciousness. She groaned, squinted around, peered at the bedside clock and cursed under her breath. Still feeling under the weather due to a particularly nasty cold, and exhausted after yesterday's late-night opening at the library, she had crawled into bed without bothering with a bath and had fallen asleep the instant her head hit the pillow – and without remembering to set the alarm.

Now she would have no time to sort out fresh clothes for today. Grabbing yesterday's blouse and skirt from where she had carelessly let them drop, she forced them on, dashed into the bathroom to splash her face with water, and dragged her hair into a straggling ponytail. Washing it would have to wait. But then, what did it matter? Nobody would notice. Nobody ever did.

"Don't you want any breakfast, love?"

"Sorry, Auntie May, I've no time. I'm late as it is. I'll get a coffee when I get to work."

"You shouldn't go out without breakfast, love!"

"It's all right, thanks. I'll take an apple with me."

Hastily stuffing the apple into her handbag, Emily grabbed her coat and headed through the front door. She knew what her mother would say if she saw her eating it on the way to work. Alice had very fixed ideas about what did and did not constitute *bad manners*, and one such terrible social no-no was eating in the street.

Emily gulped down the last bite of the apple just as she approached the library. Hastily tossing the core towards the litterbin outside, she narrowly missed hitting a young fair-haired man who was wandering past, apparently deep in thought. Emily opened her mouth to apologise, but then realised that a piece of peel had infuriatingly wedged itself between two of her back molars. As her tongue struggled to dislodge it, she realised that she hadn't had time to clean her teeth either. She made a mental note to go out at lunchtime and buy a toothbrush. It was probably worth having a spare one to keep in her desk drawer.

Always assuming, of course, that she would soon have a desk at all…

Banishing the rumour of cutbacks to the back of her mind, she hung up her coat, tucked her handbag under the desk, draped her cardigan over the back of her chair, and turned her attention to the trolley of recently-returned books.

"Good morning, Emily!"

She instantly recognised the voice and turned to smile at the speaker.

"Morning, Mr Sykes. The paper's over there, on the table. I'll just switch the photocopier on."

"Thank you, fair lady!"

Emily smiled again. She liked Mr Sykes, who treated her with such old-fashioned gentlemanly charm. In some ways, he almost seemed like the grandfather that she'd never had. Poor man, she thought, he'd had such a hard time. Utterly devoted to his wife, he had taken early retirement to nurse her when she'd been left crippled after an accident.

Ever since her death two years earlier, he had slowly begun to pick up the pieces of his own life. One of his mainstays was to come to the library every morning, take a photocopy of the crossword from that day's edition of *The Times*, and settle himself in the reference section with a pencil, a rubber, and as many dictionaries as he needed to complete it. From time to time, when the library was quiet, Emily would wander over to him, glance over his shoulder and ask how he was getting on. But she could never make head nor tail of the clues, much less how he had ever arrived at the answers. It was one of life's great mysteries.

She handed Mr Sykes his photocopied crossword, returned to the trolley, and cast her eye over the motley selection of titles. You could find out a lot about people from the books they borrowed – and sometimes it was quite a revelation. Over the past two weeks alone, the Deputy Head of the local primary school (who Emily reckoned must be pushing sixty, and she wasn't even sure from which direction) had taken out *A Beginner's Guide To Skydiving*. The vicar's wife had borrowed *Living With Depression* (whose depression, Emily wondered – hers or his?). And only the previous day, a nervous-looking youth from the bank across the road had requested *How To Prepare And Present Your Own Defence Without A Solicitor*. Goodness only knew why he wanted that. Emily tried to give him the benefit of the doubt by telling herself that he might be borrowing it for someone else, but even so, she did allow herself to heave a secret sigh of relief that he didn't work for her bank.

Amongst this latest batch of returned books were such compelling reads as *Dinosaurs – Fact Or Fantasy?*, *Mastering Esperanto In Three Months* (what a waste of time that must be, Emily thought – even if you devoted your whole life to mastering it, who on Earth, literally, would you find to talk to?), and an extremely well-thumbed and dog-eared copy of *How To Enjoy Great Sex After The Menopause*. She wondered idly who might have taken that out. Given the average age of much of the library's readership, it would probably be far easier – and quicker – to work out who hadn't.

Emily picked up an armful of the books and began returning them to their rightful places on the shelves. She was about halfway through the task when she caught sight of a young man waiting patiently at the apparently unstaffed front desk. She looked around for her colleagues, but Brenda was helping another customer, and Karen was nowhere to be seen. Oh well, she thought, I'd better go and see what he wants.

As she approached the desk, her eyes took in that the newcomer was tall and slim, that his blond wavy hair formed a perfect frame for his finely-chiselled features, and that he was casually dressed in jeans, a pale blue open-necked shirt, and a bomber jacket made of soft black leather. On closer inspection she also realised, with a sickening lurch of the stomach, that this was the same young man whom she had almost assaulted with her apple core. She prayed that he hadn't recognised her.

"Good morning. Can I help you?"

His clear blue eyes twinkled as his face creased into a smile.

"I hope so. Do you have any books on tracing family history?"

His voice was strong but gentle. Emily found herself thinking that it was the sort of voice which might read the Shipping Forecast in the small hours; the sort of voice which made one feel that however bad the storms might be, somehow all was still well with the world.

"Yes, we do. If you'd care to come this w—"

She broke off as her gaze followed his to the book in her hand. To her horror, she realised that she was still clutching *How To Enjoy Great Sex After The Menopause*.

Dropping the book on to the desk as though it burned her fingers, she spun round and began walking away, desperately hoping, as she led the way through the maze of shelves, that her blushes hadn't spread round to the back of her neck.

"What sort of thing are you looking for?" she asked, in a last-ditch attempt to cover her embarrassment and sound professional.

"Well, the truth is, I'm not really sure."

Oh no, she thought. I hope he isn't another of those time-wasters who expect us to do all the work for them.

"You see," he went on, almost apologetically, "I've never tackled anything like this before, and I really don't know where to start."

At this, Emily softened a little. She turned to face him and smiled.

"Well, if you're an absolute beginner, these ones here would be good to begin with. They explain how to get started from scratch, and once you've worked your way through the basics they'll give you some pointers about where to go next."

"Thank you very much." Those clear blue eyes twinkled into a smile again.

As Emily opened her mouth to reply "You're welcome," she found that something seemed to have happened to her breath. Her answer came out as little more than a mangled squeak.

Oh Heavens, she thought, as she left him browsing the shelves. Whatever must he think of me? First of all I throw an apple core at him. Then he finds me brandishing a book about sex in middle age, and now I can't even get my words out. And what a sight I must look, what with being full of a cold, not having washed my hair or cleaned my teeth, and still in yesterday's clothes.

She sighed inwardly. Forget it, girl, she told herself sternly. What does it matter what he thinks of you, anyway? He's probably already spoken for. And even if he isn't, he still looks way out of your league.

***

It wasn't until about twenty minutes later that it occurred to Emily that the polite and well-spoken stranger hadn't reappeared. Perhaps she ought to make sure that he was all right. Purely for professional reasons, of course, she told herself. After all, it would never do to find that he had fainted between the shelves and lain undiscovered for ages, would it?

7

Just think of the dreadful publicity for the library if that were to happen…

Picking up a pen and paper from her desk in order to give some air of respectability to her errand, she made her way back to the Family History section. After all, she told herself, even if he was still there, there would be no reason why she shouldn't be looking for something else for another customer, would there? She glued her eyes on a row of underwhelming-sounding titles as though the rest of her life depended on finding the answer to a particularly obscure query, then cautiously peered round the edge of the shelves towards the section where she had left him browsing.

He was nowhere to be seen.

She stifled an illogical and unexpected pang of disappointment and turned back towards the front desk, her imaginary quest now redundant and forgotten.

As she wandered past the entrance to the reference section, she caught a low murmur of male voices. Peering in, she saw that the well-spoken young man was now seated at the same table as Mr Sykes. He had taken off his jacket and draped it over the back of his chair, and the two of them appeared to be deep in conversation. Maybe they knew each other. Emily's pang of disappointment was replaced by an equally illogical and unexpected lifting of her spirits. She wondered briefly whether to go across and talk to them (after all, she often went to speak to Mr Sykes), but decided that it would probably be rude to interrupt them.

And anyway, as Alice had so often drummed into her, it would never do for her to appear too forward. *Nice Girls Don't Do That.*

Much good it did me, Mum, Emily thought, trying to live up to your standards of being a "nice girl".

Get a grip, she scolded herself. All that was years ago. She would not think about that dreadful business with Ben.

She settled back in her chair and began sorting through the

latest batch of request cards. Top of the pile was another one from the vicar's wife. This time she had asked for *Coping With Comfort Eating* and *How To Lose Seven Pounds In Seven Days.* Emily winced. She could only wonder what this poor woman must be going through. And it must be like living in a goldfish bowl. However rotten she might be feeling, she couldn't be seen to be not coping.

But then, that was probably true of all those who had lived through the war. It had certainly been one of Alice's many mantras: *If you can't cope, you must be doing something wrong.* Emily sighed. The war had a lot to answer for. Even now, nearly forty years after it had ended, it could still cast long shadows over the next generation.

"Excuse me?"

Emily jumped at the sound of the strong but gentle voice, almost knocking over her chair as she leapt up.

"Yes?"

"How many books can I take out?"

"How many tickets have you got?"

"Ah. Good question…"

"Are you a member?"

"Er – no."

"Just a moment."

She ferreted around in one of the drawers and pulled out a yellow form.

"If you could fill this in with your details, please, I can sort you out with some tickets. How many would you like? You can have up to four fiction and six non-fiction."

"Oh! I might as well have the lot then, please." His face again creased into that disarming smile, and Emily found herself smiling back.

"Do you need a pen?"

"Yes please, if you've got one."

He took the proffered ultra-cheap, standard, library-issue ballpoint and leaned casually over the desk towards her as he began filling in the form. Emily felt her cheeks burning and turned away hastily, under the convenient pretext of looking for new library cards for him. As she sorted four green and six blue blank cards from the drawer, she noticed, out of the corner of her eye, that he appeared to be left-handed.

"Here you are!" He straightened up and handed back the form and the pen.

"Thank you. Now, if you'd like to go and choose your books, I'll write out your tickets."

"I've already chosen them. These four here, please."

"Oh! OK then. Er – if you could just give me a moment…"

"That's fine. No rush."

Emily took the pen and began the laborious task of transferring the necessary details from the yellow form to the green and blue cards. Normally, she would have just filled out the four tickets which he needed straight away, leaving the others to be completed in a quiet moment later on. But she found herself wanting to keep him there for as long as possible. And in any case, he didn't appear to be in any great hurry to leave.

The form told her that his name was Carl Stone, that he lived in a small village just outside Medford, and that he had been born in March 1952. That made him just thirty – almost exactly four years older than she was. She wondered what he did for a living. It was certainly odd that he should be able to come to the library at his leisure during normal office hours. And it was still term-time (though only just), which ruled out the possibility of him being a schoolteacher. It also struck her as very unusual that someone only just out of his twenties should show any interest in researching family history. In Emily's experience, that was something which people generally started doing once they'd retired.

"There you are, Mr Stone. Four books, and six spare tickets. The books are due back two weeks today, but if you find you need them for longer, you're welcome to renew them provided nobody else has reserved them."

"Thank you." He smiled at her again, and again she caught her breath. "You've been most helpful."

And then he was gone. It was only after the library doors had swung closed behind him that Emily wondered if perhaps she should, after all, have told him that he could renew the books by phone, without needing to come back to the library in person. She took a deep breath and returned to her work, trying unsuccessfully to ignore the growing feeling that she desperately wanted an excuse, however feeble, to see him again.

***

By one o'clock, Emily was absolutely ravenous. Normally she made herself a packed lunch and brought it to work, but today she knew she would have to ignore the expense and go to the café across the road. She consoled herself with the old adage that one was always supposed to feed a cold. She opted for the Soup-and-Sandwich special deal, then settled herself at the only vacant table and began to eat.

"Excuse me – is this seat taken? I'm sorry to intrude, but there doesn't seem to be anywhere else to sit."

Emily looked up. The library's newest member was standing next to her table, holding a tray bearing four library books and a plate of steaming lasagne. Momentarily unable to answer because her mouth was full (*the height of bad manners*, according to Alice), she shook her head and gestured towards the empty chair. He smiled gratefully and sat down.

"Sorry," she said, as soon as she had finished her mouthful.

"That's all right. Even library staff need to eat!" Those blue eyes twinkled again. Emily smiled, flattered that he appeared to have remembered who she was.

"Thanks! And no, you aren't intruding."

Damn, she thought. I shouldn't have said that.

There was no point in trying to justify it by telling herself

11

that she was only trying to be polite; Alice's preaching seemed to ring constantly in her ears. *Nice Girls Don't Talk To Boys.*

Emily was suddenly aware that her new lunch companion was speaking again.

"Do you often eat here?" he was asking, as he picked up his fork. "I've never tried it before. Is it any good?"

Oh well, she thought. He's asked me a question. The least I can do is answer it. I don't see how anyone – even Mum – could object to that.

"I don't normally come here at lunchtime. I normally bring sandwiches and have them at work. Or in the park, if it's fine. But today I overslept and didn't have time to make any." She smiled sheepishly. "But when I have been here, for a treat, I've never been disappointed. Their home-made soups are always very nice. How's the lasagne?" she found herself adding conversationally, as he took a cautious mouthful.

He chewed for a moment, then nodded appreciatively.

"Mmm. I'd give that nine-and-a-half out of ten."

"Why? What has it done to lose the last half-mark?"

He laughed. "Nothing. The lasagne is delicious. It's just that I never give ten out of ten for anything."

"Why ever not?"

"I'm too much of a perfectionist. In my line of work, I have to be. Not that I've ever achieved it, though!"

"Why? What do you do?"

"I'm a session musician."

"Oh!" Emily looked up in surprise. Whatever answer she might have been expecting, this was certainly not it. "Forgive my ignorance, but what exactly does that involve?"

"Recording sessions, mostly. Backing tracks for soloists; incidental music for adverts, TV programmes, soundtracks, that sort of thing."

"It sounds fascinating. Have you worked with anyone famous?"

"One or two that you might have heard of." He smiled

12

again. "It's mostly fairly unglamorous work, though. Most of the time they just present us with the music and expect us to get on with it."

"Don't you need time to practise it first?"

He laughed again.

"As if! We're lucky if we get ten minutes to look over it. So long as we can sight-read, they don't usually mind. They don't necessarily want it done well – they just want it done now!"

He laid aside his fork and extended his hand across the table.

"I'm sorry, we haven't been properly introduced. I'm Carl Stone." He grinned. "But of course, you already know that!" He nodded towards the pile of library books.

Emily hesitated. But he seemed pleasant enough – and anyway, Alice wasn't there to disapprove. She smiled, took the proffered hand and shook it. It felt warm and strong. A musician's hand.

"Lovely to meet you, Carl. I'm Emily Fisher. Oh – excuse me a moment, please!" She reluctantly withdrew her hand and frantically rummaged in her bag for a tissue, then turned aside, sneezed, then blew her nose as delicately and discreetly as she could. "Sorry. I've got a stinking cold." She turned aside and quietly blew her nose again. "That was one reason why I overslept, to be honest."

Carl smiled sympathetically.

"There are some pretty nasty things going around at the moment. As a matter of fact, I'm just getting over one myself. That's why I've got a few days off – the studio manager told me to rest until I'm fully rid of it. If I can't sing or play, I'm about as much use as a chocolate fireguard."

Emily chuckled. He did seem to have a good way with words. It suddenly dawned on her that she had been happily chatting to him for a good few minutes, and it didn't feel wrong or awkward. Perhaps nice girls could talk to boys after all?

"I hope you don't mind my asking," she ventured after a moment's pause, "but why are you interested in family history?"

"It's a long story. No, I don't mind you asking, but I don't want to bore you…"

Emily smiled.

"I wouldn't have asked if I thought it might bore me!"

Carl smiled back.

"Very well then."

He drew a deep breath, as if summoning up the courage to continue.

"My grandfather died about six months ago…" He paused; his face had become serious. This was evidently a painful subject for him.

"Oh! I'm sorry to hear that. Were you fond of him?"

Carl nodded sadly.

"Yes, we were very close."

Emily sighed.

"You were lucky then. I never knew either of my grandfathers. One died when I was three, and I don't know anything at all about the other one. He died long before I was born, and my mother's never talked about him."

"That's a pity. I'm sorry."

"Thanks. But do go on – sorry for getting sidetracked."

"Well, when we were clearing out his stuff, we came across some old papers. And it appears that there's a bit of a mystery about his past."

Chapter Two

"Oooh!" Emily looked up excitedly. "What sort of mystery?"

"We'd always thought his surname was Stone – like my dad's and mine. But amongst those papers, we found a very old passport of his. And on that, it appeared that his name wasn't Stone. It was Stein. And what's more, he wasn't even English. He'd been born in Holland, in a place called Eindhoven."

"Gosh! Didn't your dad know about this?"

Carl shook his head.

"No. Dad was just as surprised as I was. Grandpa had never mentioned it. And we've no idea why not. So we decided we'd try to find out what happened."

"Hence the books?"

"Yes. But that elderly gentleman in the library who was doing the crossword..."

"Mr Sykes?"

"Is that his name? I'd taken some of the books across to one of the tables, to try to decide which ones to take out. He was sitting there with his crossword and he saw me looking at them, and we got talking. Anyway, he seems to know quite a bit about researching family history, and he's offered to give me a hand with it. He asked me to bring some of the stuff into the library tomorrow so he can have a look at it. I hope that's okay?" he added, in a concerned tone. "I don't want to be a nuisance..."

"Of course it's okay," Emily hastened to reassure him. "The library is a public building! Well, for now..." Her voice trailed off. She bit her lip and stared into her soup.

"What do you mean?"

"It's just that there's been talk that it might have to close. Or at least, cut back on staff."

"What? Why?" Carl sounded shocked.

"Council spending cuts. Or rather, 'retrenchment measures'." Emily made imaginary inverted commas in the air with her fingers. "That's what they prefer to call it. As though by giving it a fancy name, they can somehow make it seem less bad."

"Do you think it's likely to affect you?"

"I really don't know. At the moment, nobody's quite sure what's going to happen. The council don't seem too keen to tell us. But they've got three other libraries – in Littlefield, Upton and Wellbeck – and I wonder if they might be thinking that it's too expensive to keep all of them going. It's also been mentioned that if Medford Library does manage to stay open, the system will be computerised, which I suppose will mean there'll be less work for the staff in any case."

"That might be the theory, but personally I wouldn't bet on it. We've just started to use computers for some stuff in the studio, but in my experience so far, they seem to generate more work, not less. It isn't helped by the fact that they operate on the GIGO system."

"GIGO? What's that? Is that something you use in the studio?"

Carl laughed.

"Well, I suppose so – up to a point. But it isn't confined just to us; it's the same for all computers. GIGO stands for Garbage In, Garbage Out. Computers are very clever at doing what they're told, but they're only as good as the information that's put into them."

"How do you mean? Sorry to sound ignorant, but I know absolutely nothing about computers. All this is completely new to me."

Carl thought for a moment before answering.

"Well, to give a simple example: if someone told me to put my shoes and socks on, I'd understand what the concept of 'shoes and socks' meant. So, I'd put my socks on before I put my shoes on. But if I told a computer to put its shoes and socks on, that's precisely what it would do. In that order. It would put its shoes on first, and then put its socks on – over its shoes. Hence: Garbage In, Garbage Out. If you put in a rubbish command, you get a rubbish result!"

Emily chuckled.

"I can't begin to imagine how a computer would cope with some of the queries we get!"

"What sort of queries?"

"Well, only last night – at two minutes to eight, just before we were due to close – we had a man come in and ask us to find a book which he'd seen somewhere a few months ago. He couldn't remember the title or the author, and he only had a very vague idea what the book was about. The only thing he could remember for certain about it was that the printing on the pages was blue."

"Really?"

"Really. I kid you not."

"And did you manage to find it for him?"

Emily smiled enigmatically. "It's 'under investigation'."

"Meaning?"

"In theory, we're still looking."

"And in practice?"

"No."

Carl's eyes twinkled. "Do let me know if you ever find it. I haven't read a book with blue printing since I was at school."

Emily's face lit up. "Which book was that?"

"My school atlas. Sorry. I don't somehow think that's what he'd be looking for!"

Emily laughed softly.

"That's a pity. For one glorious moment I thought we might have found it!"

"No such luck! Look, we'd better get on with our lunch before it goes cold!"

They finished eating in companionable silence. As a waitress appeared and cleared away their plates, Emily glanced at her watch and leapt to her feet.

"Sorry, I must dash. I was almost late this morning. I don't want to make matters worse by being late this afternoon as well!"

"See you tomorrow, then?"

"What? Oh yes – see you tomorrow!"

She gathered up her coat and bag and scuttled out. Only when she was back at her desk did she remember that she hadn't bought a spare toothbrush.

Stinking cold or no stinking cold, she thought, I must make sure I make a bit more of an effort tomorrow.

***

Carl's eyes followed Emily as she left the café, crossed the road, and disappeared into the library. The place was quieter now, as most of the lunchtime customers had left. He ordered a coffee, sat back, and took stock of what had just happened.

What a stroke of luck that was, he thought.

After leaving the library he'd made his way across the road to the café, ordered a large mug of coffee, made himself comfortable at a table in the corner, and started to browse through his selection of books. But his thoughts had kept wandering back to the girl at the desk.

What a fascinating girl she was, with her curious dark eyes, black hair and pale skin. And she seemed so polite, so helpful, so modest. He smiled as he remembered the episode with the book she'd been holding. And she was genuinely interested in what he had to say. So very, very different from Lorna.

He'd already been looking forward to seeing her again the following day, when he was due to go back to the library for his meeting with the kind elderly gentleman, and he was wondering how he could possibly come up with some plausible-sounding excuse to talk to her.

That was when the café door had swung open and she had walked in. He'd surreptitiously watched her order her lunch and take it to the only table which wasn't already occupied. He hadn't been intending to have his own lunch there, but on the spur of the moment he'd quickly drained the remains of his coffee and gone back to the counter. Then he'd ordered a portion of lasagne and made his way to her table, hoping that all the other tables would remain full so that he could have a valid reason for asking if he might join her.

On this occasion, fortune – which so famously favours the brave – was on his side. Here was a heaven-sent opportunity to talk to her in a normal, everyday situation, and with no loss of face on either side if it didn't work out.

And now, half an hour later, he knew her name and that she didn't seem to object to his company. Beginning to form a plan for the following day, he finished his coffee and made his way back to the counter.

"Excuse me, but do you do sandwiches to take away?"

"Yes, sir. What filling would you like?" The waitress gestured towards the list chalked on the blackboard on the wall.

"Oh, sorry. I don't need one now. I was thinking about tomorrow." And praying for good weather, he added mentally. "What time do you open in the morning?"

"Half past eight. We do a very good early bird breakfast deal, if you're interested, sir. Any time up to half past nine. If you order a bacon bap, you get a mug of tea free."

Carl smiled appreciatively.

"Mmm, that sounds very tempting. See you in the morning!"

***

"Are you feeling any better now, love?"

"A bit, thanks. At least it wasn't late opening tonight!" Emily

19

forced a smile as she hung up her coat.

"And it's Thursday tomorrow," Auntie May beamed. "And then Easter. A lovely long weekend! Anyway, how was your day? Any more news about the cutbacks?"

Emily grimaced.

"Not that I know of."

A frown crossed Auntie May's pleasant features.

"It really isn't fair on you, keeping you in limbo like this. I wish they'd get on and make their minds up."

"Don't we all," Emily sighed. "Do you need any help with the meal?"

"No thanks, love, it's a casserole so it's all done. But you can lay the table if you like. Ruth and Matthew are coming."

"Okay. What time will they be here? Have I got time to wash my hair first? I meant to do it this morning but there wasn't time, and now I feel really grubby."

"Yes, go on. Do you want to have a bath, too? They won't be here for about half an hour, so you've got plenty of time. I'll give you a shout when they get here."

Emily set out five knives, forks and glasses on the table, plus a water jug and two serving spoons, then made her way upstairs and began to run the bath. She gratefully peeled off her work clothes and stepped into the welcoming warm water.

As she shampooed her hair, she once again reflected how fortunate she was in having such a kind aunt and uncle. Auntie May and Uncle Bert had loved her like a daughter – nurturing her through A-levels, supporting her through university, and afterwards taking her back into their home, saying she was welcome to stay there for as long she needed until she could manage to get a foot on the property ladder. They reluctantly agreed to allow her to pay them a modest contribution to the food bills, but otherwise insisted that she should save towards a deposit on a place of her own.

But what good would all that do now, she thought bitterly, if she was about to lose her job?

She wrapped her long hair, turban-style, in a thick towel, then lay back in the water and closed her eyes. Her mind immediately conjured up the unexpected vision of a pair of twinkly blue eyes grinning at her from a disarmingly handsome face. She smiled back into those imaginary eyes. As far as she could tell from their brief meeting, this young man Carl seemed genuinely friendly and honest.

But then, so had Ben – at the beginning.

And so, come to think of it, had Tony.

Emily's smile faded. Ben and Tony inhabited a part of her memory which she rarely visited.

Alice had never liked Ben. She had forced herself to be polite to him – provided, of course, that Emily followed Alice's strict directive of regarding him as *only a friend*. And the fact that Emily had met him at the youth club, which was run by the local church, appeared to give him some slight semblance of respectability. But even so, Emily knew exactly what her mother's thin pursed lips and steely eyes really meant. She recognised The Look from her childhood. Alice would never chastise her in public, but that silent expression always spoke volumes: *I won't say anything now, but just you wait till we're on our own…*

At the time, Emily had thought that Alice had just disliked Ben as an individual. But as time wore on, she began to wonder if Alice's objections were to Emily socialising with boys in general, rather than with Ben in particular. Looking back over her childhood and early teenage years, she was shocked to recall the number of times she had heard Alice say: *[So-and-so] is a nice girl, isn't she? She's not interested in boys…*

It was strange, though, how it seemed perfectly fine for boys to show an interest in Emily – so long as Emily wasn't similarly interested in them. *Nice Girls Don't Talk To Boys.*

Perhaps it was Alice's disapproval that had given the relationship with Ben a kind of Romeo-and-Juliet feel; a bitter-sweet, forbidden-love type of frisson. With hindsight, Emily realised that this was one of the things which had blinded her to Ben's obvious faults. The other factor had been her own total lack of contact with boys during her formative years. She had no brothers (and only one, much older, male cousin), and into the bargain had gone to an all-girls school. As a result, when she had first met Ben, she had fallen – hook, line and sinker – for his good looks, his smooth talking, his flattery, his attention, and the thought that someone as dashing, handsome and worldly as him might be attracted to someone as quiet, insignificant and inexperienced as her.

She knew now, of course, that she had been a victim of her own sixteen-year-old innocence. Any girl who had even an iota of experience of males would never have been taken in by Ben in the first place. Afterwards, when Ben had left for university and swanned out of Emily's life just as casually as he had swanned into it, she realised that she would probably have seen through him much sooner if she had managed to keep her eyes fully open. As it was, she had seen only what her young and vulnerable heart had wanted her to see. And what it really did not want her to see was what Ben ultimately wanted of her. In the end she had had a very narrow escape, though her self-esteem had taken a near-fatal blow.

She had studiously avoided boys after that, much to Alice's ill-concealed delight. No questions were ever asked, but Emily fervently hoped her mother had never worked out the whole story.

And as for Tony...

Alice had never known about Tony. He had suddenly blustered into Emily's life during her second year at university. Like Ben before him, he had been dashing, handsome and smooth-talking. He had swept Emily off her feet, and for two glorious terms had made her walk on air. Then, just as suddenly, he had pulled the magic carpet from under her, by calmly introducing her to his long-term girlfriend from his home town.

Emily had managed to keep up an appearance of dignified silence until she had escaped back to her hall of residence. Once she had locked herself safely in her room, she had sobbed bitterly for half the night and eventually cried herself to sleep. The following morning she had stared through red and swollen eyes at her blotchy reflection in the mirror above her washbasin, and firmly told herself: Face facts. You'll never be good enough for anyone, so there's no point in even trying any more.

Then, she had turned her back on any form of male society, and immersed herself in working for her degree.

A couple of years later, after she had graduated with a very creditable 2:1 and moved back to live with Auntie May and Uncle Bert, there had been that brief business with Matt's friend Gordon, whom she had met at Matt and Ruth's wedding. Gordon was a maths teacher, and Ruth always referred to him as "Geeky Gordon". He was the quiet academic type, and had been pleasant, considerate and friendly, but there had never been any spark between them.

Matt, who was genuinely fond of both Emily and Gordon, had hoped that they might get together and had been sorry that nothing had ever come of it. But Emily never saw Gordon as anything more than *only a friend.*

Alice, she reflected with a wry smile, would be proud of her.

***

Emily's thoughts, as if of their own accord, returned to Carl. Her heart fluttered as she recalled his twinkly clear blue eyes, his handsome features, the easy way his left hand had glided across the paper as he filled in the library form, his disarming smile, the warm pressure of his hand across the table at lunch, his strong gentle voice, his parting words: "See you tomorrow, then…"

Stop it, she told herself, as she climbed out of the bath and began to dry herself. Okay, so he wasn't wearing a wedding ring,

23

but for all you know, he might be happily married with four kids. And anyway, it's Mr Sykes he's coming to see tomorrow, not you. Be polite to him, but no more than that. Don't risk it. You'll only end up getting hurt.

On a practical level, she wondered what Mr Sykes would have to say about researching family history. This, in turn, made her realise how little she knew about her own family's past. Alice never spoke about it, other than periodically preaching about what a hard life her own mother had had after she had lost her husband. Emily had once asked what had happened to him, but Alice's response had been to burst into tears and rush out of the room. After that, Emily had known better than to attempt to broach the subject again.

And her dad had only briefly alluded to his own father, who had died before Emily was old enough to retain any memories of him. She had a vague recollection of having once seen a photograph of a distinguished-looking gentleman with a shock of white hair, and being told, "That was your Granddad," but once again, any more information was conspicuous by its absence.

"Emily? Are you ready? Ruth and Matthew are here. Can I serve it out?"

"Yes, I'll be down in a minute."

She pulled on her jeans and a clean T-shirt, carefully combed out her hair and spread a dry towel around her shoulders. Auntie May wouldn't mind in the least if she came to the table with wet hair. That was yet another example of the striking difference between the two sisters. They could, Emily realised, have been the original models for the proverbial chalk and cheese.

How very different my life might have been, she thought, if Auntie May had been my mother…

Chapter Three

"That was delicious, Mum. What did you put in it?"

Auntie May smiled enigmatically.

"It's a new recipe, Ruth. I haven't tried it before, so I'd no idea what it would be like. I'm glad it seems to have turned out all right."

"What's it called?"

"Cock-oh-van."

"It tasted more like chicken and mushrooms in red sauce to me." Uncle Bert's dark eyes twinkled as he winked at Emily.

"I think there might have been a dash of red wine in it as well." Emily grinned back at him. She turned to her aunt and opened her mouth to ask, but was distracted by Matt suddenly waving his hands in the air.

"Guess what, Em?"

"What?"

"Gordon's getting married."

"What?" Ruth spluttered into her drink. "Not Geeky Gordon?"

Out of the corner of her eye, Emily saw Auntie May and Uncle Bert chuckle.

Mum would never laugh, Emily thought, if I said anything like that. She would give me The Look, then lecture me later about *nice girls* and *bad manners*. Why did she always take everything so seriously? Come to think of it, I don't remember her ever seeing the funny side of anything.

"The very same," Matt went on. "It seems he's found someone who's prepared to take him on. And he wants me to be best man."

"What's she like?" Emily asked. "Have you met her?"

"Not yet. I only found out today. But we're supposed to be going out for a drink with them on Saturday night. It seems that she's called Nicola, she's very brainy, and she does things with computers."

"Well, at least they'll be a well-matched pair," Ruth remarked. "Geeky Gordon and Nerdy Nicola. Just imagine what their kids will turn out like."

"Oh, come on," Emily smiled. "She might turn out to be stunningly beautiful! Just because he's a maths teacher doesn't automatically mean he can't have an attractive girlfriend."

"True," Matt admitted. "After all, Gordon did have a crush on you for ages."

Emily blushed. She would never have described herself as "stunningly beautiful".

"Well, I guess we'll find out on Saturday." Ruth briskly rose from the table, picked up her plate and Matt's, and turned to Emily. "Come on, cuz, let's go and wash some doings up."

***

Once the two girls had reached the sanctuary of the kitchen, Ruth's face suddenly became serious.

"What's up, Em? Are you all right?"

Emily managed a wan smile, touched that her cousin had not only deftly rescued her from the embarrassing dialogue at the table, but had also noticed that something else was wrong.

"Not really."

"Is it about Gordon?"

"Gordon? Oh, good gracious, no. I'm glad he's found someone at last. I hope they'll be very happy."

"What is it then?"

Emily drew a deep breath. "Has your mum told you about the library?"

"No. What about it?"

"It's a long story, and I probably don't know the half of it. But there's been talk of cutbacks. It sounds as though I might end up out of a job."

Ruth put down the plates and gave Emily a sisterly hug.

"Oh, you poor thing. But you aren't out of a job yet. And whilst there's life, there's hope. You never know, it might all come to nothing. And then you'll have wasted a good worry!"

That was typical of Ruth – always the optimist. Emily laughed softly.

"Thanks. I hadn't thought of that."

"You need an evening out. Something to take your mind off things. Do you want to come along with us on Saturday?"

Emily hesitated.

"I...I...I don't really think Gordon would want me there. And his girlfriend almost certainly wouldn't. I wouldn't want to intrude."

"You wouldn't be intruding. The more the merrier. You don't need to decide now. Just let us know. The offer's still open!"

"Thanks."

What Emily couldn't, or wouldn't, admit to Ruth – or indeed to anyone other than herself – was that what she really didn't want was to spend an evening playing gooseberry to not one but two affectionate couples. She turned towards the sink and began running hot water into the bowl.

"Do you want to wash or dry?"

Ruth rolled up her sleeves.

"I'll wash. You sort out the stuff."

Emily slowly began to clear the cluttered worktop. Auntie May might be a good cook, but she could never in a million years be described as a tidy one.

"I say, Ruth, I think we've found your mum's new recipe!"

Tucked away in a corner, half-hidden under a pile of onion skins, was an empty packet. It was labelled: "Sauce mix for *coq-au-vin*."

***

Before going to bed, Emily carefully selected the clothes she would wear for work the following day. Eventually, after several false starts, she settled on a pair of smart black trousers and a blouse in a fetching shade of cornflower blue, which she knew suited her. After all, she reminded herself, she was supposed to look smart for work. And after she had looked such a sight today, she really did need to make the effort tomorrow. This was purely for work, of course. It might even increase her chances of keeping her job. It had nothing – absolutely nothing at all – to do with trying to impress anyone who might be coming into the library as a customer.

***

Carl arrived at the café a little before half past nine, ordered the breakfast special and settled down at a table by the window, from where he could observe the door to the library. He hungrily devoured his bacon bap, but made the mug of tea last as long as he reasonably could. Just before ten o'clock, he went up to the counter to order his take-away sandwich. By the time it had been made up and packaged and he had returned to his vantage point, the library doors were already open.

It wasn't long before he spotted Mr Sykes walking across the library forecourt. Carl respectfully waited for a few more minutes before finally making his own way across the road, the bag containing his lunch in one hand and a bulging carrier bag in the other.

He strode confidently up to the front desk, fully expecting to be greeted, as he had been yesterday, by Emily. But today the desk was staffed by a middle-aged, slightly overweight woman with ash-blonde hair and gold-rimmed glasses. Carl hoped that his face didn't betray his disappointment.

"Can I help you?"

"Er, I know it sounds odd, but I'm supposed to be meeting someone here. An elderly gentleman who was here yesterday, doing the crossword."

The older woman's face cleared into a helpful smile.

"Mr Sykes?"

"Yes."

"I think he arrived a few minutes ago. He usually sits in the reference section. It's just over there, on the right."

"Thank you."

As Carl made his way towards the reference section, he peered hopefully around for Emily, but there was no sign of her. Maybe her cold had got worse, and she wasn't in today. He realised that, having missed seeing the library open its doors, he had no way of knowing for certain if she had even arrived.

Carl found Mr Sykes wandering around the reference library shelves, helping himself to a variety of dictionaries and reference books and setting them out on one of the tables. He turned and smiled as he heard Carl approaching.

"Good morning!"

"Good morning. I've brought the stuff." Carl laid the carrier bag on the table as the two of them sat down. He extended his hand. "I'm Carl Stone, by the way. I don't think I ever introduced myself properly yesterday."

The older man returned the handshake.

"Alf Sykes. Pleased to meet you!"

"I'm really grateful to you for helping me with this," Carl continued, "though I'm afraid it looks like a pretty hopeless case."

"Well, we'll find out, won't we?" Mr Sykes put his hand into the bag and cautiously drew out the contents. He perused them for a few moments in thoughtful silence. "Hmm. I see what you mean. I can probably make sense of some of this, but quite a lot of it seems to be in a foreign language."

Carl sighed. "That's what I was afraid of."

Mr Sykes smiled. "Don't worry. We'll start off with what we

can decipher, and see how much we can find out from that. Afterwards, we can… Ah, Emily! There you are!"

Carl spun round and followed Mr Sykes' gaze as Emily came across to the table, a piece of paper in her hand.

"Here's your crossword, Mr Sykes. Morning, Carl!"

"Morning." Carl smiled at her, and was pleased to notice that she smiled back. "How's your cold today?"

"Still there, but not quite as bad as it was yesterday, thanks. I expect I'll live!" She nodded towards the pile of papers on the table. "That lot looks interesting."

"It's my grandfather's stuff. Though I think it's going to be an uphill struggle trying to make any sense of it."

Emily smiled sympathetically as she turned to leave.

"Good luck!"

***

When Emily returned to the reference section half an hour later (officially for the purpose of putting away and rearranging the library's selection of daily and weekly newspapers), Carl and Mr Sykes had spread their project out over most of the table. They had made two or three separate piles of yellowing papers, and were sitting side by side, poring over the documents and making notes. In the middle of the table lay a dark green leather folder and a small black leather box.

"How are you getting on?" she asked, in what she hoped was a casual tone, as she began to stow the newspapers away on the shelves.

Carl looked up. "Very slowly!"

"Have you managed to find anything yet?"

"Only that my grandmother was born in Dorset!"

Emily smiled. "Well, it's a start, I suppose! How did you find that out?"

"From this." Carl held up a piece of paper. It was cream and pink, about fourteen inches long and about eight inches high, and covered in black copperplate handwriting. Emily came across to the table.

"What's that?"

"It's my grandmother's birth certificate."

"We've decided to start with the English documents," Mr Sykes added.

Emily took the certificate from Carl, then frowned as she peered at it more closely.

"How very odd."

"What's the matter?" Carl asked.

"I'm not sure. It's just that..." Emily broke off, unsure how to continue.

"What?"

"My birth certificate doesn't look anything like this."

"What do you mean?" Mr Sykes asked gently.

Emily sat down at the table.

"Well, this one has all sorts of extra stuff on it. Look. Place of birth, father's name, mother's name and maiden surname, father's occupation, address of informant (whatever that means) ... And it's huge. Much bigger than mine. Mine is about eight inches square, and just shows my name, my date of birth, and the country where I was born. Why haven't I got one like this?"

Chapter Four

Now it was Mr Sykes' turn to look puzzled.

"How very strange," he murmured, almost to himself. He thought for a moment, then added, "Were you born overseas, Emily?"

Emily shook her head.

"No. My birth certificate just says that I was born in England. But I've lived in Medford all my life, so I presume I must have been born somewhere round here. I've never really thought about it before." She stared thoughtfully into space.

Carl, sensing her apparent discomfort, decided to change the subject. He reached across the table and took back the birth certificate.

"What does 'informant' mean?" he asked casually, turning back to Mr Sykes.

"It's just the person who first registered the birth." Mr Sykes looked at the certificate again. "In your grandmother's case, you can see here, it was her father. And the birth certificate also gives us the address of where they were living at the time. That's the same address as the one in the 'Place of Birth' column – so from that, we can see that she was born at home."

Emily smiled.

"You seem to know a lot about this, Mr Sykes."

The old man's eyes twinkled.

"Well, I have been doing it for years, on and off!"

"How far back have you managed to trace?" Carl asked.

"Quite a long way – so far, at least. I've got back to around 1800 with one branch of the family, and a little further back than that with another."

Carl whistled under his breath.

"That's pretty impressive! Have you found any skeletons in the closet?"

Mr Sykes grinned.

"One or two."

"Oooh! What sort of skeletons?" Emily asked, intrigued.

"I found one ancestor who ended up in prison for assaulting a policeman. And another who I think might have been a bigamist, but I haven't so far been able to prove that for certain. Though it seems that bigamy was much more common than most people realise."

"Why would that have been, do you think?"

"Probably because it was very difficult to get a divorce in those days."

Emily nodded.

"That would figure, I suppose."

"But one of the biggest shocks I had," Mr Sykes went on, "was when I discovered my grandparents' guilty secret."

"What was that?" Carl and Emily asked, in perfect chorus. They looked at each other and laughed.

Mr Sykes chuckled.

"Well," he went on, "my grandparents celebrated their Golden Wedding when I was fourteen. I remember it particularly because I'd just left school a couple of months earlier. And it was quite a party – they'd had nine children altogether! But years later, when I started researching the family history and looked for a record of their marriage, I couldn't find it."

Emily raised her eyebrows.

"How intriguing!"

"It was indeed. But then, quite by chance, I found it – and that was when I realised that I'd been looking in the wrong place."

"What do you mean?" Carl asked, equally intrigued.

"I'd based my calculations on the date of their Golden Wedding party, so I'd subtracted fifty years from that and searched the marriage records for that year. But it seems that they hadn't got married when I thought they had. The day and the month were right, but the actual date of their marriage was a whole year later. It seemed that they'd celebrated their Golden Wedding a year early."

Carl whistled under his breath.

"How strange! Have you any idea why they might have done that?"

"Oh yes!" Mr Sykes grinned conspiratorially. "It all became clear when I started to check the birth records. My Uncle Sam was their first child, and their Golden Wedding party was a very respectable sixteen months before his fiftieth birthday. But if they'd celebrated in the correct year, it would have become obvious to the whole family that they'd only taken four months to produce him!"

"So, they had their Golden Wedding a year early, just to hide..." Emily blushed.

Mr Sykes grinned again.

"I think the correct terminology is 'pre-marital conception'!"

Emily managed a weak laugh. Carl quickly turned to Mr Sykes.

"How did you first get started on your research?"

"I started just after my wife's accident. There was a lot of reading and letter-writing involved, so it was a good way of passing the time at home. She helped me a lot with it, too. My only regret is that I didn't get started on it sooner, whilst my parents were still alive."

"What makes you say that?"

"Well, there's no substitute for first-hand information. The best way to go about it is to start with the present, with what you know, and gradually work backwards. I knew a little bit about my parents' generation, obviously, but now I really wish I'd thought to ask them – and my grandparents – more questions, before it was too late."

"Me, too," Carl sighed. "I wish my grandfather could be here now, to explain all this lot."

Mr Sykes grinned sympathetically.

"But," he went on, "as I've found, even first-hand accounts aren't necessarily reliable. If there's a lesson to be learned from that Golden Wedding story, it's that you should never make any assumptions that what you've been told is true. You should always double-check it!"

Emily glanced at her watch and reluctantly rose from the table.

"I suppose I'd better get back to work," she sighed. "But do let me know if you need anything."

"Thank you. We will." Carl's blue eyes twinkled again as he smiled up at her. She returned the smile. Just out of politeness, of course, she reminded herself. In exactly the same way that she would be polite to any of the library's customers.

But none of the other library's customers could make her heart leap when they looked at her. "Just being polite" to Carl was certainly not going to be easy.

Chapter Five

By lunchtime, the English side of Carl's family tree was starting to take shape, and the two men decided to take a break before tackling the more difficult overseas papers in the afternoon. Mr Sykes seemed quite happy to stay and keep an eye on the documents whilst he turned his attention to the crossword over his packed lunch. Eating in the library was, strictly speaking, not permitted, but he assured Carl that this would not be a problem.

"I've done it before," he whispered conspiratorially. "Many times. And I'm very discreet – nobody has ever noticed. I'll be fine. You go and get a breath of fresh air."

Carl was grateful that his wish for good weather appeared to have been granted. The spring day was bright, if not particularly warm, but it was probably as much as one could expect for early April. He picked up his sandwich bag and headed for the park, not really knowing what he would find there. Fortunately, it wasn't long before he spotted Emily sitting eating her lunch on a bench by the duck pond. He couldn't help thinking that she looked sad, or possibly worried. At any rate, she was lost in thought and did not see him approaching.

"Hello. Is this seat taken?"

She glanced up. Her face lit up as she recognised him, although, as on the previous day, he had once again caught her with her mouth full. She nodded towards the seat on the bench beside her.

"This is getting to be a habit!" he grinned, as he sat down and unwrapped his sandwich.

"So it would seem!" she answered, as soon as her mouth was empty. "How's the research going?"

"Very slowly. I had no idea how long it would take to make sense of even the most basic bits of it. But your Mr Sykes seems to know what he's doing, thank goodness. Tackling it on my own, I wouldn't have known where to start."

"So, how far have you got?"

"Well, just on the basis of my grandmother's birth certificate, we've already got back as far as one set of great-grandparents. It seems that there's quite a lot of information on birth certificates — it's just a matter of knowing how to interpret it."

"Except on mine," Emily sighed.

"Yes, that is strange. Why don't you ask your parents about it?"

"My parents are both dead," Emily said flatly, staring at the ground.

Carl choked on his sandwich.

"Sorry," he said lamely, once he had found his voice again.

Emily turned to look at him, though neither her face nor her voice betrayed any kind of emotion.

"That's all right. You weren't to know."

"What happened? Was it an accident?" Carl asked gently. "Though if you don't want to talk about it, I'd quite understand."

Emily hesitated for a moment before answering.

"They were both killed in a car crash."

"When? Recently?"

Emily shook her head.

"No. It was just under nine years ago. I was seventeen."

"Were you in the car with them?" Carl shuddered. He realised, with a lurch of the heart, that he couldn't bear the thought of her being injured.

"No, I was at school when it happened. My gran had an appointment at the eye hospital. She would have been perfectly happy to get the bus, but my mum insisted that that would be

'too much trouble' for her, and that she ought to go by car."
Emily sighed. "That was typical of my mum. She was forever
dancing attendance on Gran, even though Gran never asked for
it. Mum always claimed that Gran needed looking after –
though Gran always said she was happy looking after herself."

"So why was your dad there, too? Wouldn't he have been at
work?"

"Normally, yes, he would. But Mum didn't drive, so of
course Dad had to take the day off and play chauffeur. Gran
never forgave herself. She said afterwards that if she'd stuck to
her guns and gone on the bus, it would never have happened."

"So your gran survived the crash?"

"She wasn't in the car. It happened when they were on their
way back, after taking her home. A car coming the other way
was overtaking on a blind bend, and hit them head-on. They
were killed instantly." Emily paused. "But at least they didn't
suffer."

She stared into space. It was Carl who eventually broke the
silence.

"Emily, I'm so sorry. I had no idea…"

She turned to face him. As her dark eyes looked straight into
his, he could see no reproach, no anger, no bitterness – just
understanding and compassion. And possibly a hint of
something else; something indefinable, something which made
him catch his breath.

"Don't worry," she said softly. "As I said, you weren't to
know. And I'm sorry if I made you feel uncomfortable just
then. It happened so long ago that I suppose I've got used to it
by now, and sometimes I forget that not everybody knows
about it."

"So, what happened to you afterwards?" he asked gently.
"You were seventeen, you said?"

Emily nodded.

"I went to live with my aunt and uncle."

"For how long?"

"I'm still living with them now. I'm trying to save up to get a place of my own, but it's a slow process. But hey, that's more than enough about me," she added brightly. "Tell me more about the research."

Carl didn't answer immediately, as he had just taken another mouthful of his sandwich. As he chewed, it struck him again, with full force, how different Emily was from Lorna. He had just put his foot in it – right up to the thigh – but in those beautiful dark eyes he saw no blame, no anger, no recriminations... And then she had just drawn a line under the whole episode. *That's more than enough about me...* He could never, in a month of Sundays, imagine Lorna ever saying anything like that.

"There seems to be quite a lot of stuff to sort through," he said at last, grateful for the opportunity to talk about something different. "And quite a lot of it looks as though it's in Dutch."

"Dutch? Well, I suppose that's to be expected, if your grandfather was born in Holland."

"Mmm," Carl nodded thoughtfully. "But unless we can find someone who understands Dutch, I think that side of it's going to be a complete non-starter."

"How much more is there of the English stuff?"

Carl considered for a moment.

"Quite a bit, I think. That should keep us occupied for a while, anyway, even if we can't get anywhere with the Dutch side."

He took the last mouthful of his sandwich, keeping back a little of the crust, then rose from the bench and shook the crumbs from his lap.

"Have you finished?"

Emily nodded.

Carl held up the remains of his lunch.

"Do you need to go straight back, or have we got time to go and feed the ducks first?"

She glanced at her watch, then looked up at him and smiled

happily.

"That would be good."

***

The ducks swam eagerly towards them as they approached the edge of the pond.

"They seem very tame, don't they?" Carl remarked.

"Yes, they always are. I think they must associate humans with food."

"Do you know anything about birds?"

"Not a great deal. I like to watch them though, and if I see one I do like to know what it is."

"So what have we got here, then?"

Emily looked around.

"Well, those are swans…"

"Yes, even I had managed to work that out!" Carl smiled self-deprecatingly. "What about those?"

"Mallards. The ones with the green heads are the males, and the brown ones are the females."

"And those? The ones which look as though they couldn't make up their minds what colour they wanted to be?"

"Mandarins, I think – though I'm not absolutely sure. I'll have to look it up later."

"So what about that one over there under the tree?"

Emily followed Carl's pointing finger.

"The white one with green and orange patches and the funny little crest?"

"Yes."

"I've no idea. I've never seen one like that before."

Carl peered at the mysterious duck again.

"It looks almost as though it could be a cross between a mallard and a mandarin," he said, after a few moments. "Is that possible, do you think?"

Emily thought for a moment.

40

"I've no idea. Though I agree it does look like it." She laughed softly. "Maybe they've been misbehaving!"

She silently cursed herself as soon as the words were out. *Nice Girls Don't Say Things Like That.* Now he'll think I'm being too forward, she thought. And to add insult to injury, it hadn't even been a particularly funny thing to say.

She turned her face away, pretending to look back at the ducks so that Carl wouldn't see her embarrassment. But she was relieved to hear that he appeared to be laughing as well – even if, as she suspected, he was only doing so out of politeness.

***

"Who was that young man?" Brenda asked Emily, when she was back at her desk and Carl had gone back into the reference library. The fact that the two of them had returned to the library together had evidently not escaped the older woman's notice. Emily knew from experience that she would have to choose her words carefully. Brenda was a lovely person and a delightful work colleague, but she did have an unfortunate tendency to put two and two together and get the answer forty-seven.

"I think he's a friend of Mr Sykes. I met him outside just now, when I was on my way back from lunch."

Fortunately, Brenda seemed satisfied with this oblique and non-committal answer.

"Oh yes. I don't think they can have been friends for very long, though! I remember him arriving first thing this morning, but he just asked for 'the man who was doing the crossword yesterday.' It sounded to me as though he didn't even know Mr Sykes' name! Anyway, what on earth are they doing? They've been in there all morning!"

"I'm not sure exactly. They seem to be looking at old papers or something."

"Oh well, if you do ever find out, I'd be intrigued to know!"

Brenda replied, as she turned back to her desk. "Oh, by the way, the vicar's wife came in while you were out at lunch. There's another book request from her."

She handed over the card. Emily read it and her eyes widened.

"Did she say where she'd heard about this?"

"She said she'd read about it in the *Courier* last week."

Emily looked again at the title on the card, and frowned.

"Is this all she gave you? No author, or publisher, or ISBN?"

Brenda shook her head.

"No, just the title."

"Well," Emily remarked pragmatically, "I suppose even that's a big improvement on that one the other evening."

"Oh, the 'blue printing on the pages' chap? I think he might have a long wait for that!"

"Any idea how we go about trying to find this one?"

Brenda thought for a moment.

"We could try contacting the *Courier*, I suppose."

Emily's nodded. "Well, I suppose that would be a good place to start. Did she say which day it was?"

"Sorry, no. And I never thought to ask her. But they should all be over there." Brenda jerked her head in the direction of the reference section. "Would you mind going and having a look through them to see if you can find it? I'd do it myself, but I really need to sort out the other requests."

"No, I don't mind," Emily answered brightly, trying to conceal her delight at having a valid excuse to go back to Carl and Mr Sykes. "It might take a while, though," she added, almost as an afterthought.

"That's all right. Take as long as you need. Shall I bring you a cup of cocoa when it goes dark?"

Emily laughed.

"I hope it won't take that long!"

Although, as she made her way back to the reference section, she secretly hoped that it would.

She carefully extracted all the copies of the *Courier* for the previous week from the shelves, then carried them over to the table next to where Carl and Mr Sykes were sitting. The two men were hunched over the piles of papers and scratching their heads. Carl looked up and smiled as he heard her approaching.

"How are you both doing?" she asked conversationally.

"Not very well, I'm sorry to say. And I don't think we're going to get any further with this lot." Mr Sykes picked up the top paper from one of the piles on the table and handed it to her. "At least, not unless we can find someone who understands Dutch."

Emily glanced idly at the piece of paper in her hand, then looked more closely as her eyes focused on the printing.

"Just a minute…"

"What's the matter?" Carl asked.

Emily squinted at the old document in silence for a few moments, then her face cleared. She sat down next to Carl and spread the paper out on the table in front of her.

"I don't think this is Dutch."

Carl stared at her.

"What do you mean?"

"Well, I don't understand any Dutch, but I can read this. Or at least, I can recognise some of the words. This isn't Dutch. It's German."

Chapter Six

"German? How do you know?"

"I did German A-level," Emily answered modestly.

"So, can you tell us what it says?" Mr Sykes asked eagerly.

"Not all of it, sorry, I can't make out all the handwritten bits. But the big word at the top, in that strange Gothic script, is *Trauschein*. If I remember rightly, I think that means marriage certificate. Just hang on a moment, I can check."

She crossed to where the foreign language dictionaries were stored, extracted a thick red tome from the shelf, and brought it back to the table.

"I'm not sure if this dictionary is completely up-to-date, but I don't suppose that will matter for looking up something like this." She flicked through the book and ran her finger down the page.

"Yes, here we are. *Trauschein* – certificate of marriage."

Carl and Mr Sykes exchanged looks.

"Can you work out whose marriage certificate it is?" the older man asked.

Emily studied the document again.

"The groom – *Bräutigam* – was Wilhelm Josef Stein, and the bride – *Braut* – was Monika Hannelaura Schmidt. And they married in Hamburg on the eighteenth of November, 1899."

Carl whistled under his breath. "Wow, that's amazing. Well done!"

"Thanks, but it was nothing."

"No it wasn't! We're a lot further on than we were five minutes ago!"

Emily blushed modestly.

Carl picked up the marriage certificate and looked carefully at the names.

"Stein, you said?"

"Yes."

"Hmm. That's the name we found on my grandfather's old passport."

Emily's face cleared.

"Of course!"

"Of course what?" Carl asked, still puzzled.

"Stein is German for stone. So that must be where your English surname came from."

"So you reckon my grandfather's family is German, rather than Dutch?"

"I couldn't say for certain, but it's beginning to look like it. Well, partly, at least. Though it still doesn't explain why your grandfather was born in Holland."

Carl sat still for a few moments, deep in thought.

"What were their first names again?" he asked eventually.

"Wilhelm and Monika. Wilhelm is the German form of William."

"Hmm. I seem to remember my grandfather once mentioning that his father was called Bill. Could these be his parents, do you think?"

Mr Sykes' face lit up.

"You know, Carl, I think we might be on to something here!" He turned to Emily. "So what about the rest of the papers? Could you take a look at those, too?"

Emily's face fell.

"I'd love to, but I need to get on with this. Sorry." She gestured towards the adjacent table.

"What's that?"

"I need to find something in one of these newspapers."

"What are you looking for?"

Emily sighed.

"A needle in a haystack."

"What sort of needle?" asked Mr Sykes, with a twinkle in his eye. "A sewing needle? A knitting needle? A crewel needle? A bodkin?"

Emily looked at him in amused surprise.

"You seem to know a lot about needles!"

Mr Sykes grinned.

"My wife used to do a lot of knitting and sewing when she was alive. And towards the end, when she couldn't do much else, it kept her happy. When she was confined to a wheelchair, I often used to take her out to the handicraft shop. They sold stuff which I never knew existed, and eventually I got to be quite an expert on the finer points of haberdashery! But seriously, Emily, what are you looking for?"

Emily explained about the strange book request (though without being specific about who had made it), and how their only hope of tracking down the book was to find the relevant article and then contact the *Courier*.

"Can we help you look?" Carl asked.

"Oh, I wouldn't dream of putting you to any trouble..."

"It's no trouble," Carl assured her firmly. "And anyway, you've already been a tremendous help to us. So the very least we can do is try to help you."

"Absolutely." Mr Sykes nodded in agreement.

Emily hesitated. Could she really turn down such a generous offer?

"Well, if you really don't mind... Though I must be honest with you, I don't think it's going to be very easy to find. I don't even know exactly what I'm looking for. It might be a book review, or it might be an advert, or it might just be mentioned in an article somewhere..."

"All the more reason," Mr Sykes interrupted firmly, "why three people should tackle it rather than just one. Many hands – or in this case, eyes – make light work. But it's a complicated title. Could you write it down for Carl and me, so we know exactly what we're looking for?"

Emily happily complied. But even with all three of them working on the task, it still took nearly half an hour of intense searching before Carl finally struck gold. The details of the book were tucked away in the middle of an extremely learned-sounding article in the edition for the previous Thursday. Emily smiled at him gratefully as she made a note of the details.

"Thank you. Thank you both very much. I don't think I'd ever have found it on my own."

"You're most welcome." Carl smiled back at her in a way which made her heart flutter. "But I'm sure you would – though I agree that it might have taken a bit longer." He looked again at the title of the book. "Though goodness only knows why anyone in their right mind would want to read this."

Emily laughed nervously.

"To be perfectly honest, I'm more worried about whoever it was who wrote it in the first place. I mean, for one thing, how would they go about researching it?"

The two men looked at her, then at each other, and both shuddered.

"Yeuchh," Carl spluttered.

Mr Sykes winced.

"Yeuchh, indeed. The mere thought of it has been enough to put me off my tea."

***

"Brenda? I've got it. Do you want to ring the *Courier*, or shall I?"

"You do it. You've done all the work; you may as well have the moment of glory!"

"Thanks." Emily smiled sheepishly. She hadn't done all the work, and she certainly hadn't found the information herself, so she didn't feel that she deserved either the praise or the moment of glory. But then she added, as if it had only just occurred to her, "Oh – and I've managed to find out what Mr Sykes and his friend are up to."

"Yes? What?"

"It seems that Mr Sykes is helping him to research his family history. But they're having a bit of difficulty with it, because a lot of the papers appear to be in German."

Brenda raised her eyebrows thoughtfully.

"You know German, don't you?"

"Well, I wouldn't exactly say 'know.' I did it at school, but I don't think I've actually spoken any since I did my A-level Oral!"

"But you can still read it, can't you? Why don't you go and see if you can help them?"

"Well, I…"

"Go on. It's not too busy in here at the moment; nothing that Karen and I can't manage between us. And we know where you are if we need you."

"But does it count as 'correct use of library resources,' or whatever they call that policy these days?"

Brenda thought for a moment before answering.

"I don't see why it shouldn't. After all, the library is supposed to be a source of information. If someone came in and asked you a research-related question, it would be part of your job to help them find the answer. I don't see that this is any different. And anyway," the older woman's face brightened, "it might even give us more ammunition to throw at the council, to convince them that they need to keep all of us on here."

"Oooh, I hadn't thought of that! Okay then – I'll go and see if there's anything I can do for them. But I'd better ring the *Courier* first."

***

"Back again, Emily? What are you looking for now?"

Carl looked up as Mr Sykes spoke. Emily's heart began to

flutter when she saw how his face lit up when he saw her. She managed, not without difficulty, to keep her voice steady.

"Do you still want me to have a look at your other stuff? It's pretty quiet this afternoon, so I might as well try to do something useful."

"Do we still want you to look at it?" Mr Sykes repeated, grinning widely. "Can a duck swim?"

Emily stopped in her tracks.

"I haven't heard that expression for years. It's something my dad used to say."

She caught Carl's gaze. The compassion she saw in those clear blue eyes, as he evidently remembered their conversation in the park, made her heart race. But she looked away quickly and turned her attention back to the paperwork on the table.

"So," she began, forcing herself to attempt to sound professional, "where do we start?"

"I think you're probably best qualified to decide that," Mr Sykes answered. "You at least have some idea what these papers might be!"

"Well, I wouldn't be too sure about that, but here goes!" Emily pulled the pile of papers towards her and began to look through them.

"Did you manage to get in touch with the *Courier*?" Carl asked.

Emily nodded. "I rang them, but they didn't manage to give me an answer straight away. They were very helpful, though. They're going to look into it and ring us back when they've found it. But they did warn us that they might not be able to get back to us until tomorrow. I just hope that the person who asked for that book isn't in a desperate hurry for it."

"I still can't get over why anyone would ever want to read a book like that," Mr Sykes murmured, shaking his head.

"Or, as you said earlier, Emily, why anyone would even want to write one," Carl added. "There must be some pretty weird people out there."

"We get some pretty weird people in here sometimes," Emily sighed. "Or at least, people who make some pretty weird requests."

"Aye, lass," Mr Sykes replied, putting on an incongruous Northern accent. "There's nowt so queer as folk!"

Emily and Carl stared at him.

"It's something my grandmother used to say," he added, reverting to his usual voice. "She came from Lancashire and worked in the cotton mills. She was right, though – people can be very strange. But just think how dull life would be if everyone was normal!"

Emily, recalling how 'normal' her own cloistered upbringing had been, couldn't help silently agreeing with him.

Chapter Seven

"Carl, you said your grandfather was born in Holland?"

Carl nodded.

"What was his first name?"

"Nicholas."

"Do you know what year he was born?"

Carl considered. "Well, he was seventy-eight when he died, and that was last October, so…"

Emily did the sum on her fingers. "1904?"

"No, his birthday was in December. He was nearly seventy-nine. So, 1903."

"Just out of interest, what date in December?" Mr Sykes asked.

"The sixth. Why?"

"I just wondered. December 6th is the feast of St Nicholas. If I remember rightly, I read somewhere that the Dutch make quite a big fuss of St Nicholas. So that could be why he was called Nicholas."

Carl looked up in surprise.

"Well, I never knew that!"

Emily looked up from the paper she was holding.

"Did he have any brothers?"

"No."

"Are you sure?"

Carl thought for a moment, then answered cautiously, "I never met any, and he never said anything about having any. Well, not to me, at any rate."

"Just because he didn't mention it, that doesn't necessarily mean it didn't happen," Mr Sykes said thoughtfully. "Why do you ask, Emily?"

"Well, this paper here is headed *Geboorte Certificaat*, and I think this is one which might well be in Dutch. It certainly isn't German – at least, not the type of German I was taught – but *geboort* is very similar to the German *Geburt*, which means birth. And *certificaat* looks pretty self-explanatory. So could it be a Dutch birth certificate, do you think?"

Mr Sykes nodded. "That would make sense."

"But," Emily went on, "if your grandfather was called Nicholas, then this birth certificate can't be his." She peered again at the old handwriting. "I can't understand all of this, but I think I can just about make out the key words. The birth seems to be of someone called Hans Wilhelm Stein, born in Eindhoven, Holland, on the seventh of April, 1900. The parents are Wilhelm Josef Stein and Monika Hannelaura Stein. There's a short word next to the mother's name which looks something like 'gob'. Oh hang on, no – it's 'geb'. In German it would be short for *geboren*, which means born. Oh yes – the next word is Schmidt."

Emily looked up and her eyes shone.

"So this must be the same couple as are on that marriage certificate we were looking at earlier. If they were your great-grandparents, then this Hans Wilhelm Stein must have been your grandfather's elder brother."

Carl sat in silence as he took it in. Meanwhile Mr Sykes, who had been listening intently to what Emily had been saying, picked up the Steins' marriage certificate from the table and looked at it again.

"Emily, could I have a look at that, please?" He held out his hand for the birth certificate, studied it for a moment, then laid the two documents side by side on the table.

"Well, it seems as though I'm not alone in having ancestors who got married in a hurry!"

"What?" Carl shook himself out of his reverie.

"Look here. Date of marriage, November 1899. Date of birth, April 1900. Subtract one from the other, and you get an answer which is rather less than nine months!"

"Well, that might explain why they left Germany," Carl mused.

"Not necessarily," Mr Sykes answered. "True, they might have had to leave Hamburg, particularly if they wanted to avoid any risk of scandal. But to move to a totally different country – well, that does seem a bit extreme. There might well have been another reason why they went to Holland – something not connected with the 'pre-marital conception'."

"What sort of reason, do you think?" Carl asked.

Mr Sykes opened his mouth to answer, but was distracted by Emily's sudden exclamation as she picked up the birth certificate and looked at it again.

"Look!" she gasped. "Look at the date!"

"What about it?" asked Mr Sykes.

"He was born on the seventh of April. So today would have been his eighty-second birthday!"

Carl stared at her as light dawned.

"It would still be his eighty-second birthday," he murmured, "if he's still alive out there somewhere…"

Chapter Eight

"It's odd, though, especially if Hans is still alive, that your grandfather never mentioned him," Mr Sykes went on, after a moment's pause. "That could be for any number of reasons. Perhaps he just didn't mention him – for reasons which we will probably never know. Perhaps they somehow became estranged. Or they might just have lost touch. It happens, even in families with the very best of intentions, if someone moves away. Or perhaps," Mr Sykes' voice became more serious, "Hans died a long time ago, possibly in tragic circumstances, and your grandfather never mentioned him because he found it too upsetting to think about."

"What sort of tragic circumstances?" Emily asked, in an unsteady voice.

Carl looked quickly at her. The care and concern in his eyes made her knees turn weak. She was glad that she was already sitting down.

Fortunately Mr Sykes, deep in thoughts of his own, seemed unaware of the sudden tension.

"Well," he answered eventually, "if Hans was born in April 1900, he would have turned eighteen in April 1918. That would make him just about old enough to have fought at the end of the First World War."

"For which side?" Carl asked excitedly.

"That's a very good question," Mr Sykes answered slowly. "Germany, I suppose..."

***

Emily turned back to the pile.

"Carl, have you ever seen your grandfather's birth certificate?"

Carl shook his head.

"Not that I know of. Though, of course, if it looks anything like that one you just found, it's perfectly possible that I have seen it but not known what it was."

"Well, at least we now have some idea of the kind of thing we're looking for–"

She broke off as a flustered-looking Brenda appeared in the entrance to the reference section. She was followed by two men in overalls, each one carrying a large metal appliance, about eighteen inches square and eighteen inches deep, and with a plain matt glass screen. A third man was following them, pushing a porter's trolley on which a metal chest of drawers was precariously balanced.

"Could you put them over there on the table for the moment, please?" Brenda was saying. "I'll need to work out exactly where they need to go."

Emily excused herself from Carl and Mr Sykes, and made her way across to her colleague.

"What's going on? What are these things doing here?"

Brenda sighed in exasperation.

"These aren't ours. But it seems that the library in Littlefield is closing for a couple of weeks for stocktaking, so the council is bringing all their local studies stuff here for the time being."

"What? Why didn't they tell us beforehand?"

Brenda frowned, then looked furtively around before lowering her voice to a whisper.

"It seems that they did – last week. But when the letter arrived, it appears that it was Karen who opened it. When I asked her about it just now, she said she got distracted and then forgot to pass the message on to us."

"Is Karen all right?" Emily asked in a low voice. "I haven't seen her for ages."

"I'm not sure," Brenda answered, equally quietly. "She certainly doesn't seem like her usual cheerful self at the moment."

"Excuse me, ladies," one of the workmen coughed discreetly. "Where would you like these to go?"

"What? Oh, sorry." Emily turned and smiled apologetically. "Well, they'll need a power supply, of course." She glanced around. "Where are the nearest sockets?"

"Over there in the corner, I think."

For the next few minutes, under Brenda's direction, the two men installed the machines on a large table on the far side of the room. As they positioned the chest of drawers alongside it, Brenda sat down at the table and switched the machines on.

"Well, they both seem to work okay. That's a relief."

"Excuse me, but what are they for?"

Brenda turned round to find that Carl and Mr Sykes had appeared at her side.

"They're the microfiche readers for the local studies centre," she explained. "We seem to be looking after them for a couple of weeks. But, looking on the bright side, it might mean we get a few more people through the doors whilst we've got them."

"Are these the birth, marriage and death records?" Mr Sykes pointed eagerly to the chest of drawers.

"Yes. And the census records, up to 1881."

Mr Sykes turned to Carl and Emily. "I think," he said excitedly, "that the task is just about to become much, much easier!"

"That may be, Mr Sykes," Brenda smiled, "but I'm afraid your task, whatever it is, is going to have to wait. I know time flies when you're having fun, but it's five-to-five and we'll be closing in five minutes."

***

"I don't quite understand," Carl said, as they hastily packed up the papers from the table. "What exactly do you mean about the task getting easier? What's in those drawers?"

"They're microfilm lists of the births, marriages and deaths from 1837 onwards. Those two machines are for reading them."

"Why 1837? That seems an odd sort of date."

"That's when it became compulsory for all births, marriage and deaths in England to be officially registered," Mr Sykes explained. "Though I very much doubt that we'll need to go back as far as that."

"So how exactly is it going to help?" Emily asked.

"It's a bit complicated to explain. It will be a lot simpler if I can just show you how the system works and talk you through it. I'll show you tomorrow."

"Okay. See you in the morning, then?"

Mr Sykes nodded, picked up his hat and headed for the door.

"Thanks for everything," Carl called after him.

Mr Sykes turned back and smiled.

"My pleasure, young man!"

Chapter Nine

"I don't know about you," Carl sighed, as he picked up the bulging carrier bag, "but I'm absolutely gasping. Are you in a rush to get home, or have you time for a cup of tea first?" He jerked his head in the general direction of the café across the road.

Emily hesitated. But then she realised that she, too, was desperately thirsty, and that a cup of tea would be most welcome. There was no insinuation in Carl's voice – he just wanted a cup of tea, and he had asked her if she wanted one. That was all there was to it, she told herself firmly. Nothing more, nothing less. It would be impolite to refuse, wouldn't it?

She smiled gratefully.

"A cup of tea would be lovely. Thank you. Can you just give me a couple of minutes? I can't really leave before five."

"Okay. Shall I go and order it, and see you over there?"

"Yes, all right. Thanks."

"Do you want anything to eat with it?"

"No thanks. But don't let me stop you, if you want anything."

Carl tucked the bag under his arm and headed for the door. It was only after he had left that Emily spotted that the small leather box, which she had previously noticed on the table amongst all the papers, was now lying upside down on the floor. She picked it up and put it into her handbag.

By the time she had made her way across the road to the café, Carl was already installed at a small table in the corner. In front of him was a tray bearing a large pot of tea, two cups and saucers, a jug of milk, a sugar basin, and a plate with two large shortbread biscuits.

"The biscuits came free with the tea," he explained, in answer to Emily's questioning look. "It seems that they have a special deal if you order before five o'clock. I scraped in with about thirty seconds to spare!"

Emily sat down opposite him, opened her handbag and took out her purse.

"How much do I owe you?"

Carl held up his hand as if to stop her in her tracks. It came so close to hers that she could almost feel its warmth. She dropped her purse on to the table, and clumsily drew her hand away under the guise of picking it up again.

"Nothing. This is on me."

"But–"

"No buts! It's just a small way of saying thank you for helping us this afternoon."

"But you helped me, too, with looking for that book title."

"Did the *Courier* ever ring back about it?"

"Not that I know of, though the girl I spoke to did say that they might not be able to get back to us today, so I'm not really surprised."

"I suppose they're rushed off their feet at the moment, with all the extra news reports about the Falklands," Carl mused.

"Mmm. I hadn't thought of that…"

Carl lifted the lid off the teapot and peered inside to inspect the contents.

"This looks as though it should be ready to pour. Do you like it weak or strong?"

"Not too strong, please."

"OK, I'll pour yours first. There. Does that look like a good colour?"

"That looks just right, thanks." She helped herself to milk as Carl filled his own cup.

"Sugar?" He pushed the sugar basin towards her.

"No thanks."

"Sweet enough?"

Emily smiled wistfully. "That's what my dad used to say."

"Oh yes?" Carl's face became serious. "Look," he went on awkwardly, "I'm really sorry about earlier."

"When? What do you mean?"

"At lunchtime. When I put my foot in it about your parents."

"What? Oh, that..." Emily smiled reassuringly. "Please, forget about that. As I said before, it doesn't matter. And I'm sorry, too. I shouldn't have been so abrupt with you. As it was, I wasn't in the best frame of mind, so I probably sounded as though I was angry. And I wasn't. Well, not with you, anyway."

Carl smiled. "Well, that's a relief! But what was bothering you? Who were you angry with?"

Emily sighed. "Not so much 'who' as 'what'. I'm just worried about work, that's all."

Of course, it wasn't all. Not by any means. But she could hardly tell him what was really bothering her – that his smile made her heart turn over, that the sound of his voice made her catch her breath, that he made her go weak at the knees just by looking at her, and that when his hand had come so close to hers just now, she had desperately wanted to reach out and grasp it and draw comfort from its strength and warmth. But of course, *Nice Girls Don't Do That.*

And in any case, he was a successful musician, and she was just a humble library assistant who probably wouldn't even be that for very much longer. It was hopeless. She hadn't been good enough for a couple of rotters like Brutal Ben or Two-Timing Tony, so what chance did she have of being remotely good enough for a decent guy like Carl? There was no point in even thinking about it.

She realised he was speaking again.

"I wish there was something I could say to make you feel

better."

Oh Carl, she thought, if only you knew. You could cure it all with just one word. Or rather, with three words...

She sipped her tea, to give herself time to compose herself and think of something suitable to say in reply.

"I was talking to my cousin about it last night," she said eventually. "And she told me not to worry about it, because it might never happen. She said there was no point in wasting a good worry."

Carl chuckled.

"That's a good way of looking at things. I must remember that one for one of the studio technicians. He's a terminal pessimist."

"Oh crikey. He must be a real misery to work with."

"Well, not really. He likes his job, and he's very good at it, but it's just that he always expects that something will go wrong. His philosophy is 'a pessimist is never disappointed'."

Emily laughed gently.

"My dad once said that you should always borrow from pessimists, because they never expect to get it back."

Carl chuckled again.

"I must remember that one, too, next time I need to borrow a fiver."

"Only a fiver? If you know he isn't going to expect it back, why not make it a tenner?"

Carl's clear blue eyes twinkled.

"That's better!"

"Better than what?" Emily asked, as she drained her cup and put it down on the table.

"Better than having you looking sad." He nodded towards her empty cup. "The cup that cheers! Ready for a top-up?"

"Yes please."

"So, you have a cousin, you said?" Carl asked, as he refilled her cup.

Emily nodded as she picked up the biscuit.

"Two, actually. There's Ruth, my aunt's daughter. But she doesn't live with us any more. She's five years older than me, and married. And there's her older brother, Graham, but he lives up in London, and we don't see him very often."

"Have you...any brothers or sisters?" Carl asked tentatively.

"No," Emily answered, taking care to draw out the vowel, so that the word didn't sound too brusque or abrupt. "But that was probably just as well," she added lightly. "I think there were times when my mother must have thought that even one child was more than enough."

Carl smiled. "I find that hard to believe. What makes you say that?"

Emily hesitated. How much should she tell him?

"It's difficult to explain," she answered, after a moment's pause, "without sounding disloyal to my mother. But basically, everything was fine so long as I played by her rules. But the moment I stepped out of line..." Her voice trailed off.

Carl looked at her steadily. "Go on," he said gently.

"I...I had a boyfriend when I was in the Lower Sixth. My mother never liked him. It caused no end of rows."

"What happened to him?"

"He finished with me when I..." The next words stuck in her throat. No, she couldn't tell Carl the whole ugly story. "... When he went off to university," she added lamely. "He said he didn't want to be tied down."

That, at least, was true as far as it went.

"And was your mother pleased when he left?"

"Oh yes, there was no doubt about that. And in a way that made it a lot worse for me, because even though it felt like the end of the world at the time, I knew that I couldn't let myself be seen to be upset about it in front of her. So I tried to keep out of her way as much as possible." Emily stared down into her teacup. "I know I was being pretty impossible to live with. But I thought I had plenty of time to make it up to her. But then..." She bit her lip. "Then there was the accident. All of a sudden, she wasn't there any more. And I'd never had the chance to tell her I was sorry..."

"And you went through all that when you were only seventeen?" Carl said softly.

"It does sound a bit melodramatic, doesn't it? Sorry, I didn't mean to burden you with all that."

"It didn't sound melodramatic at all. I'm just amazed at how much you've been through. I'm nearly twice the age that you were at the time, and I'm not sure how I'd cope with something like that even now." Carl paused, then smiled wistfully. "But Grandpa often used to say that if it doesn't kill you, it can only make you stronger. Which must make you very strong indeed!"

Emily looked into those lovely blue eyes and smiled gratefully.

"Thanks. I'd never thought of it in those terms before." She paused. "I wish I could think about the work situation in the same light, though."

Carl smiled back.

"I know it's easy for me to say this, but at the risk of sounding like your cousin, try not to waste a good worry!"

"Easier said than done, but I'll try. At least, I'll try not to think about it all the time. Oh! I almost forgot." She rummaged in her handbag and fished out the little leather box. "I found this on the floor just now. I think I remember seeing it on the table earlier. Is it yours?"

"Oh gosh, yes! Thank you! I didn't leave anything else behind, did I?" Carl reached across the table as she handed it over. And this time, as he took it from her, their fingers did touch.

It happened for no more than a split second, but she felt as though an electric current had passed through her.

"No, I couldn't see anything else lying around," she answered, desperately trying to sound normal. She nodded towards the box. "What's in it?"

"Here, look." He pressed the small clasp and the lid clicked open. His hand was still tantalisingly close to hers as she leaned forward to get a better look.

Inside the box, resting on a cushion of faded velvet fabric, was a strange metal object. It was about two-and-a-half inches long and about an inch wide, and looked as though it was made of brass, although it was now darkened and tarnished. Emily peered at it closely. She could see that it bore the design of a crown, above which were inscribed the words *Gott mit uns*.

"Is that German, too?" Carl asked.

"Yes. *Gott mit uns*. It means, literally, 'God with us'."

"Have you any idea what it might be?"

"I'm not sure exactly. Was this amongst your grandfather's stuff?"

"Yes. We found it with the folder."

"What folder?"

Carl reached into the bag and pulled out the dark green leather folder, which Emily recognised as the one she had seen on the table in the library.

"This folder. We didn't get round to looking at it today, what with all the other stuff we were doing."

Emily smiled sheepishly.

"That's probably my fault, for distracting you with looking for that thing in the *Courier*."

"You seem to have forgotten," Carl grinned, "that you didn't ask us to do that. We offered. And anyway, we've still got tomorrow to carry on with all this. But it would be good to try to get the bulk of it done if we can, because after Easter I'll be back at work."

"May I see?"

The folder was about nine inches high by six inches wide, and about a quarter of an inch thick. On opening it, Emily could see that it contained several sheets of yellowing paper, all covered in neat swirly handwriting. She studied the script for a few moments, then looked up.

"This is all in German, too. It looks as though they might be letters of some kind."

"Can you tell what they say?" Carl answered excitedly.

"Well, not immediately, but given a bit of time I might be able to work out the gist of it." She looked up. "If you can trust me with borrowing this overnight, would you like me to take it home and have a look at it?"

His face, as he looked up from peering at the ancient handwriting, was only a couple of inches away from hers. She caught her breath.

"I wouldn't want to put you to any trouble," he said softly.

She could barely hear his voice over the sound of her pulse pounding in her ears.

"It's no trouble," she answered, after she had managed to recover some small vestige of the power of speech. "I've nothing else planned for this evening. And to be honest," she added brightly, "I'm finding the whole story rather fascinating!"

"Really?" His face lit up. "In what way?"

"Well, there must be some reason why your grandfather never talked about his past, not even to your father. Maybe this" (she tapped the cover of the folder) "might contain some explanation why he didn't..."

Chapter Ten

As Emily was speaking, the thought came into her mind that she had already discovered far more about Carl's family history during the course of the last two days than she had known about her own over the past twenty-six years. Perhaps, when this project was over and Carl had returned to work, she might find the time to start a similar venture of her own.

"You really wouldn't mind?" Carl was saying.

"Not in the least. Though perhaps I ought to warn you, I might not get very far with it. The handwriting doesn't look too bad, but my German is pretty rusty!"

"However rusty it is, it's still tons better than mine. I only know one word of German."

"What's that?"

"*Stein.*" That familiar twinkle came back into his eyes. "It means stone, apparently. And that's one more word of German than I knew this time yesterday!"

"Well, actually you know four words of German." Emily grinned and picked up the leather box again. "Look. Here are three more: *Gott* – that's God, *mit* – that's with, and *uns* – that's us."

Carl stared down at the metal object.

"God with us. That sounds like some kind of motto," he said thoughtfully.

Emily looked at it again.

"Is there a name anywhere on it?"

"I've no idea." Carl picked up the box, took the object out and turned it over in his hand.

"Hmm. It doesn't look as though it's got a name on it anywhere. But look – what do you make of this?"

She took it from him and studied it for a moment. On the back were two small metal lugs.

"Could it be a belt buckle, do you think?"

As she handed it back, their fingertips touched again. And this time, neither of them moved away.

"Hmm. Possibly." Carl's clear blue eyes gazed deeply into hers. "We can always show it to Mr Sykes tomorrow and ask him if he can shed any light on it."

Emily's heart leapt. She had the distinct impression that Carl was thinking as little about the spoken words as she was.

"Yes," she murmured, as she gazed back at him. "He might know something about this kind of..."

"Er – excuse me."

They both jumped as the waitress approached.

"Sorry to interrupt, but we'll be closing in five minutes. Have you finished?"

"Oh, yes, of course. Sorry." Carl packed the metal object back into its box and stowed it away in his pocket. Emily tucked the folder carefully into her handbag as they rose from the table.

"Can I give you a lift home?" he asked, as they emerged into the early evening sunshine.

Again, her heart leapt. But she forced herself to answer noncommittally.

"I wouldn't want to take you out of your way."

"Why? Where do you live? John O'Groats?"

She chuckled.

"Left to myself, I'd probably end up going that way. Geography was never one of my strong points."

"How do you normally get home?"

"I walk. It isn't far. It usually takes me about ten or fifteen minutes."

"Well, that definitely won't be out of my way."

"Where is your car?"

He grinned.

"I hope it's still where I left it this morning."

"Which is?"

"On the other side of the park. It's one of the few places in Medford where you can still park all day for free."

Without her needing to say anything, he seemed to take it for granted that her answer was yes. They began to stroll at a leisurely pace through the park, neither of them seeming to be in a tremendous hurry to reach their destination. It occurred to Emily that she was now walking in entirely the wrong direction, and that she would probably have been home in less time than it would take them to cover the distance to wherever Carl had left his car. But despite her tiredness, it was a sacrifice which she was more than happy to make, if it meant that she could spend a few minutes longer in his company.

She was almost sorry when they finally reached the car, which was parked under a tree in a shady side street. She hadn't really given much thought to what sort of car he might drive, but she still managed to be surprised to discover that it was a two-year-old Volkswagen Golf in an elegant shade of silver.

"A German car, I see!"

"Yes. Rather appropriate, under the circumstances, isn't it?" He grinned and patted the roof of the car affectionately, brushing off a few twigs which had fallen on to it during the day.

As he unlocked the car and opened the passenger door for her, she found herself recalling a girl whom she had known at university, who had always assessed the "suitability" of her potential boyfriends by the size – or rather, the price – of the cars they drove. On that basis, Emily thought, Cheryl wouldn't have given Carl a second look. As it was, many a worthy suitor had fallen at the first hurdle.

The last news Emily had heard about Cheryl was that she was in the throes of a very messy divorce, from a guy who had always been known (though never in Cheryl's hearing) as The Berk With The Merc. This news had saddened Emily (for, despite Cheryl's obvious errors of judgement, Emily had never disliked her), but equally it had failed to surprise her.

Carl carefully stowed away the carrier bag in the boot before settling himself into the driving seat. As he turned the ignition key, the car radio came on. The air was filled with the familiar, homely sound of Radio Four.

Viking, Forties, Cromarty, intoned the announcer. *South-easterly backing north-easterly four or five, decreasing three later. Intermittent slight rain. Moderate, becoming good.*

Emily leaned back contentedly in her seat.

"I always love to listen to the Shipping Forecast."

"Why?" Carl asked in amused surprise. "I've never been able to understand a word of it."

"It always sounds so soothing. Almost like a lullaby. I'm not convinced that you even need to understand it. But my dad did once explain to me what it all means."

"Oh yes?"

Emily nodded. "And it all makes perfect sense, once you know how to decode it. The first bit is—"

"Sorry to interrupt, but first of all, whereabouts do you live?"

"Oh, sorry. Hawthorn Drive. Go back down High Street, past the library, then turn left by the war memorial. Take the second road on the right – that's Hawthorn Road – then turn left about halfway along. That's Hawthorn Drive."

"OK." Carl eased the car out into the traffic. "Sorry. You were saying – the Shipping Forecast?"

"Oh yes. They have to give out a lot of information in quite a short space of time, so they don't bother with the headings every time, but just give out the details. That's why it doesn't seem to mean very much to a lot of people, but the sailors and the fishermen out there know exactly what they need to listen out for. If you listen to it carefully, you'll notice that the sections always follow the same pattern. First of all they give the name of the sea area – and those always come in the same order. That's always followed by the wind direction, then the next bit is the wind speed. After that comes the weather conditions, then the last bit is the visibility. Listen…"

Sole, Lundy, Fastnet, Irish Sea. Southerly veering south-westerly three or four, increasing five later in Irish Sea. Squally showers, becoming fair later. Moderate or good.

"Oh, I see now! How very clever!"

"It is, isn't it? And if you're near the coast, it makes a pretty reliable weather forecast, too." Emily sighed wistfully. "It always reminds me of my dad whenever I hear it. I was intrigued by it as a child, because one of the sea areas is Fisher, and I wondered why they were reading out our surname! And the one which comes after Fisher is German Bight. I think I was well into my teens before I realised that it wasn't spelled B-I-T-E. I told you I was never very good at geography!"

Carl chuckled.

"Well, you seem to have managed okay with your navigation skills today! Here we are. Hawthorn Drive. What number?"

"Number fifteen. About halfway along on the left. And thank you very much."

"Would you like a lift in the morning?"

"Well, I wouldn't want to take you out of your way…"

"It won't be out of my way. I'll be driving past the end of your road anyway."

"In that case…yes, please. That's very kind of you."

"And I hope you will let me buy you lunch tomorrow. As a thank-you for spending your evening looking at those letters."

"But you already paid for the tea. And I…"

Carl held up his hand for silence.

"No buts. My treat."

"But you might want to wait and see if I manage to make any sense of it first!"

"As I said, no buts! And that's a risk I'm quite prepared to take!" Carl grinned. "I'll pick you up at about ten-to-ten. I can drop you off at the library first, and then go and find somewhere to park."

Emily's face creased into a broad smile.

"In that case, thank you. That would be lovely. Would it be easier for you if I wait at the end of the road?"

Carl's eyes smiled back into hers.

"Okay. I'll see you in the morning!"

She watched as he turned the car round, and waved as it moved off. Only after it had disappeared round the corner did it occur to her to wonder if perhaps she might have sounded a little too eager. *Nice Girls Don't Do That...*

Chapter Eleven

Emily opened the front door just as the six o'clock news was starting on the television.

"Hello, Auntie May. Sorry I'm a bit late."

Auntie May looked up from her seat on the sofa.

"That's all right, love. I can't say I'd noticed. And anyway, you're a big girl now – you're allowed to be late once in a while!"

"Where's Uncle Bert?"

"Upstairs. He's only just got home himself. How did it go today?"

"Still no word about the cutbacks, but generally it was a bit more interesting than usual, thanks. Pretty tiring, though. We've got a couple of customers who are trying to research family history. They seem to have taken up residence in the reference library. Oh, and the vicar's wife made another of her weird book requests. That kept us busy for a while."

"Oh yes? What did she want this time?"

Auntie May's jaw dropped as Emily told her.

"Phew! That's pretty bizarre even by her standards. Did you manage to find it?"

"Mmm, yes and no. She said she'd read about it in the *Courier*, so first we had to find the article which mentioned it, then ring the paper to ask if they knew how to order it. We're still waiting for them to get back to us."

"Well, if you do ever track it down, I'd love to see it!"

"Okay. But you're not by any means the only one – the rest of us are pretty intrigued about it, too. Do you need any help with the meal?"

"No thanks, love. The chops are in the oven already, and I'll just go and put the potatoes on. It should be ready at about half past."

"Thanks." Emily sat down on the sofa and tried to concentrate on the television news. It seemed that the Navy were now on their way to the Falklands. Emily's previous knowledge of Britain at war had just come from hearsay and history books. But this was real live Britain at war, even if it was happening thousands of miles away in the South Atlantic. And these were real live people going off to that real live war, with the very real possibility that they might not come home. A sudden vision swam before her eyes of Carl in uniform, being conscripted and sent away to fight… She shuddered.

"What's up, love?" Auntie May had returned from the kitchen.

"I was just thinking about…" Her voice trailed off and she stared at the television screen. "…about those poor guys being sent off to the Falklands." She turned towards her aunt. "How much do you remember about the Second World War?"

"Enough to last me a lifetime-and-a-half," Auntie May sighed as she sat back down on the sofa. "As I expect you can imagine, given what it did to our family."

Emily stared at her.

"What do you mean? I don't understand."

"Really? How much do you know?"

"Nothing. Nothing at all."

For the second time within five minutes, Auntie May's mouth dropped open. But this time it was not in amused surprise, but in undisguised horror.

"What?" she gasped, when she had found her voice again. "You mean…you mean your mum never told you?"

***

73

As Carl drove the short distance to his own home, he thought back over what had happened in the past few hours.

What a truly lovely girl she was. Beautiful, intelligent, amusing and modest.

He really thought he'd blown it at lunchtime, with that horrendously clumsy gaffe about her parents. But she had been so understanding – *you weren't to know* – and so forgiving. Later, over the cup of tea, there had been the thrill he had felt at that momentary touch of their fingers. Had she felt it, too? As her gaze had held his own, there had been a mysterious look in those lovely dark eyes. Did he dare to hope that she might feel the same way about him as he did about her?

But he knew he was going to have to tread very carefully. He was sure, from the way in which Emily had suddenly checked herself in mid-sentence, that there must have been something pretty significant about that ex-boyfriend which she hadn't wanted to tell him. *He hadn't wanted to be tied down*, she'd said, but Carl had an uneasy feeling that there was a lot more to it than just that. Whoever that guy was, he had obviously hurt her very badly. At the very thought of it, Carl found his fists clenching over the steering wheel in involuntary rage.

But just how deep, he wondered, was the scar which that old wound had left? And could that be why she seemed to be holding back – because she was afraid of getting hurt again? Carl knew that he could not risk hurting her even more by rushing her into something which she might not be ready for – or (even worse) might run the risk of scaring her off. The thought that he might lose her was already making his blood run cold.

He swung his car into the driveway, took the carrier bag out of the boot and carefully locked the car. Unlocking the front door, he bent down to pick up the post from the doormat.

An electricity bill, a bank statement, a catalogue from a supplier of electronic components, a catalogue from a guitar supplier, a card from the dentist reminding him that he was now due for his six-monthly check-up, and a postcard from a work colleague who had taken a spring break on a sunny Spanish shore. At the bottom of the pile was a plain white envelope, bearing a typewritten name and address and an indecipherable postmark.

Intrigued, he sat down on the bottom of the stairs and opened it.

He read and re-read its contents several times. Once he had fully taken in what it said, the colour drained from his face.

How on earth was he going to tell Emily about this?

Chapter Twelve

"So, what happened?"

"You really, really don't know?"

Emily shook her head.

"My mum never talked about it. Even when I was doing World War Two at school and I asked her about it, she would never answer any of my questions."

Auntie May got up from the sofa and turned off the television. She drew a deep breath before sitting back down next to Emily, then reached out and took hold of her hand.

"Brace yourself, love. This isn't a nice story."

Oh crikey, Emily thought. What on earth was coming now? She looked up at her aunt and saw a faraway look – a look which Emily had never seen before – come into the older woman's dark eyes.

"It was in September 1942. We were living in Somerset. Your granddad had an uncle – Uncle Stanley – who had a farm not very far from Yeovil. Gran and Granddad thought we'd be safer there than in the city, and it worked out rather well because Gran and your mum were both working as Land Girls..."

"Really? I never knew that..."

Auntie May gasped. "Your mum never even told you that?"

Emily shook her head again.

"What about you?" she asked. "What were you doing whilst all this was going on?"

"I was still at school. Anyway, our father – your granddad – was in the Navy. He was home on leave, and he'd come out to the farm to see us. It was harvest time, and he offered to help with the harvest. Gran and your mum and the other Land Girls all did the day shift, and Granddad and the men went out on the night shift."

"The night shift? Sorry. I don't understand." Emily hadn't intended to interrupt her aunt again, but she couldn't comprehend the idea of harvesting at night.

"It was a full moon," Auntie May explained. "The harvest moon, I suppose you'd call it. You had to get the harvest in quickly, and when there was a full moon it was usually light enough to see what you were doing, so people harvested round the clock.

"Anyway, the farm was next to the railway, and there was a big railway junction just a little way up the line. The planes were coming back from a raid on Bristol, and one or two of them still had a couple of bombs left. It was a full moon and the pilots could see the railway track. The planes followed the railway line, then when they flew over the junction, they dropped the bombs."

Auntie May shuddered, and her voice shook as she tried to summon up the courage to carry on.

"One bomb fell in the road, the other fell into the field. There were about a dozen men and young lads working out there. They got no warning of it at all – no chance to run or take cover. When the bomb dropped, none of them stood a cat in hell's chance."

For a long moment, the two of them sat motionless; Emily staring at Auntie May, Auntie May staring back through brimming eyes into a painful and long-buried past.

"How old were you?" The question sounded inane and inappropriate, but Emily felt a desperate need to break the deafening silence.

"I was thirteen and your mum was sixteen. There was no welfare state then (that didn't come in until after the war was over), so Gran had to go out to work, taking whatever work she could find. It was usually scrubbing and cleaning – you know, the sort of jobs that nobody else wanted. She worked seven days a week, just to keep us from starving. When she got old, your mum insisted that Gran deserved to be looked after, after everything she'd done for us over the years. Your mum always seemed to do the lion's share of it, though. I often tried to help, but for the most part Alice always insisted on doing it herself."

Auntie May shook her head sadly, then looked down and bit her lip, as if struggling to continue.

"I even offered to go with Gran on the bus to the eye hospital that day, so that your dad wouldn't have to take the day off," she murmured eventually, in a voice so choked with emotion that Emily had to lean forward to catch what she was saying. "But your mum wouldn't hear of it. And you know what she was like when she'd got her mind set on something…" Auntie May's voice trailed off.

Emily sat very still. Yes, she knew exactly what Alice was like when she had her mind set on something.

"What about you?" she asked eventually.

"What about me?"

"How did you…cope?"

Auntie May smiled wistfully.

"I coped because I had to. That was what you did in those days. You just coped."

Emily nodded sadly.

"Yes, I remember my mum never had any time for anyone who couldn't cope. She always used to say, 'If you can't cope, you must be doing something wrong.' Maybe that's why she wouldn't let you help her with Gran."

Auntie May looked up.

"What do you mean, love?"

"Well, I always understood that the way she looked at it, if you needed help, it meant that you weren't coping. That was always how it came across to me, at any rate. Maybe she thought that if she asked for help, that would be an admission of weakness. And if she accepted help – from you or from anyone else – then that would an admission of failure." Emily squeezed her aunt's hand. "Whatever she thought, it certainly isn't a reflection on you."

"You know, love, I've never thought about it like that before. But you're right." Auntie May smiled gratefully. "Thank you. That makes me feel a lot better."

"Where is my granddad buried?" Emily asked after a moment.

"In the churchyard in the village where it happened. That's where they buried all the people who were killed that night. But your granddad hasn't got a headstone. Gran couldn't afford one at the time. Alice always intended that she would put one up, but…"

Once again, Auntie May's voice trailed off. The two women sat in silence for a moment.

"There's something else, though, love, that you ought to know," Auntie May went on. "A little while after all that happened, your mum–"

"Come on, girls, what's going on here?"

The two women jumped at the sound of Uncle Bert's jovial voice. But the smile died on his lips as he caught sight of their stricken faces.

Auntie May patted Emily's hand and murmured, "I'll tell you later, after we've eaten."

She rose from the sofa and motioned Uncle Bert to follow her into the kitchen, leaving a stunned Emily to take stock of what she had just heard.

Suddenly everything was beginning to fall into place. Emily could now understand why Alice had never spoken about her father or about the war – the memories had obviously been far too painful. Maybe her way of coping with them had been simply to blank them out altogether. And presumably this included her own recollections of her days in the Women's Land Army, linked so strongly as they were with the loss of her father.

And it might also go some way towards explaining why Alice

had always put her mother's needs first – not just above her own, but also (on many occasions) above those of her husband and her daughter. Could it be that she blamed herself in some way for what had happened? Did she believe, perhaps, that she should have been out in the field that night, and that her father had died in her place?

But what was it that Auntie May still had to tell her? What else could possibly have happened to her mother afterwards?

***

Emily found that she had little appetite. She tried to convince herself that it was just because of the biscuit that she had eaten with her cup of tea only an hour or so earlier. But whatever the reason, the evening meal – although cooked to perfection – was eaten in uncomfortable silence.

Auntie May had evidently briefed Uncle Bert about the gist of their earlier conversation, as he smiled at Emily sadly and sympathetically whenever she looked up and caught his eye. He was wise enough not to raise the subject himself over the meal, but after they had finished eating he stood up and announced that he would do the washing-up and make everyone a cup of tea, and that Emily and Auntie May should go and sit down. Neither woman offered even a token resistance to his suggestion.

Once back in the sitting room, Emily drew a deep breath and asked her aunt what it was that she had been about to tell her.

Auntie May took Emily's hand again.

"After your granddad was killed, Gran and I had to move back to Medford – mainly so that Gran could find work to support us. There wasn't much paid work to be had in the area around the farm. But your mum stayed on there, working as a Land Girl. A couple of months later, she came home on leave... and that was when she met Tom."

"Tom? Who was Tom?"

Auntie May sighed. "She never told you about him, either?"

Emily shook her head.

"As I said, she never told me anything, even when I asked her. So, who was this Tom?"

"Tom was a soldier. The battalion was stationed at Medford and she met him at a dance. They fell for each other straight away. Hook, line and sinker."

Emily caught her breath.

"So why didn't they..?" Her voice, and her hands, trembled. She found herself unable to finish the question.

Auntie May squeezed Emily's hand.

"They would have done, I'm sure of that. After she went back to the farm, they wrote to each other regularly, and went to visit each other as often as they could. Then, a few months later, his regiment was sent off to India. A couple of months after that, his letters just stopped. She never found out for certain what had happened to him, but nobody was left in much doubt."

The sitting room door opened and Uncle Bert appeared, carrying a tray bearing three steaming mugs of tea. Emily gratefully accepted the mug he handed to her. Uncle Bert knew exactly how she liked her tea (mild to medium strength, with a moderate amount of milk, and no sugar), so she was astonished to find the tea in her mug was the colour of burnt caramel and that Uncle Bert was offering her the sugar basin.

"Come on, love," he said, in answer to her questioning look. "I know this isn't how you normally drink it, but you've just had a bad shock. Strong sweet tea will do you a power of good. Put three spoonfuls in and stir it well."

Emily winced at the prospect, so used was she to taking her tea or coffee unsweetened, but she reluctantly complied. As she raised the mug to her lips and the steam reached her nostrils, she could detect the sweet aroma of the hot strong liquid. It did not smell at all appetising, and she braced herself as she prepared to take the first tentative sip.

Amazingly, Uncle Bert's panacea did appear to have some effect. She found that her rapid breathing was slowing down and her mind was becoming calmer.

So the war had taken not only Alice's father, but also her sweetheart. It was little wonder that she'd never talked about it. It might even go some way towards explaining why Alice had never seemed happy about Emily learning German at school, even when it had turned out to be one of her best subjects.

This thought reminded Emily of her promise to look at Carl's folder of letters. She had been intending to tell Auntie May about it, but in view of what she had just found out, she had no idea how her aunt might react. She was fairly sure that Auntie May didn't share Alice's pathological hatred of all things German, but she decided, on balance, that discretion would probably be the best of a fairly unsatisfactory bunch of options. For the time being, at least.

She finished her sweet tea and rose from the sofa.

"I think I might have an early night, if you don't mind. I'll go upstairs and read for a while."

Auntie May smiled understandingly.

"Night night, love. See you in the morning."

Once safely inside her room, Emily retrieved her German-English dictionary, which hadn't seen active service since her days in the Upper Sixth. She took Carl's folder of letters out of her handbag, untied the frayed and faded ribbon which held it closed, opened the folder and carefully picked up the first page. The paper felt cheap and coarse, yet the handwriting – although old – proved to be reasonably easy to decipher.

But she was totally unprepared for what she was about to read.

Chapter Thirteen

Carl was usually a good sleeper, but he woke several times during the course of that night. Sometimes he woke with the contents of the letter running through his mind. At other times he was convinced that he could see Emily's face smiling at him through the darkness, though whenever he tried to reach out towards her, his hand touched nothing but thin cool air.

Eventually, just after half past six, reluctantly accepting that he wasn't going to go back to sleep, he hauled himself out of bed, showered and shaved, then went downstairs to make himself an early breakfast. The letter was still lying where he had left it the previous evening, in the middle of the kitchen table.

As he waited for the kettle to boil, he picked up the letter and read through it again, wondering if he might have imagined the whole thing. But it really did say what he thought it had said. And no, it wasn't going to go away. Not without a struggle, anyway.

So, he wondered, what on earth am I going do now? Should I tell her? And if I do, will she understand? Or is it better to keep quiet about it – at least for the moment? But then, if I do go through with it, she's going to find out anyway. And what will she think of me then, if I haven't been honest with her about it all along?

Either way, could it mean the end of everything, before it has even begun?

On the spur of the moment, he opened the back door and stepped outside into the cool spring morning. After the restless night and the mental turmoil, it was, literally, a breath of fresh air. He stood on the doorstep, closed his eyes, and inhaled deeply and gratefully. A blackbird was proudly and melodiously defending its territory from the top of a nearby holly tree.

It must be good to be a bird, Carl thought. Life would be so uncomplicated. Find a mate, build a nest, and sing. Just what I want to do with my life, in fact. But will I ever manage all three? Until yesterday, I thought I might be on the verge of it, but now..?

He stepped back indoors and made a pot of tea and a couple of rounds of toast. Noticing that he was almost out of bread, he was reminded that the shops would be closed for the next few days for the Easter break. Grabbing a piece of paper and a pen, he began to write himself a shopping list. He would have to nip out of the library during the day to buy what he needed for the weekend. What a nuisance, he thought; everything stops for Easter.

It came to him in a flash. Everything stops for Easter – including the post. The letter could easily have been caught up in the Easter backlog, so he could just as easily say that he had not received it until Saturday – or even, perhaps, the following Tuesday. That would give him plenty of time to think carefully about what he should do about it, and also give him a chance to test the water with Emily. If today's lunch went well, he could then try asking her out on a proper date.

For the first time since he had received the letter, he began to feel confident about what the next few days might bring.

***

Emily had no reason to doubt that Carl would pick her up as they had arranged, but just to be on the safe side, she set off from home at her usual time of just before quarter to ten. She need not have worried; Carl's car was already waiting at the corner by the time she reached the end of the road.

"Morning!" He switched off the car radio as she settled herself into the seat.

"Morning." She couldn't help thinking that he looked rather tired. And possibly worried. "Are you all right?"

"What? Oh, yes, I'm fine, thanks. It's just that I didn't sleep very well last night."

"Oh, I'm sorry to hear that."

He turned to smile at her.

"Not to worry. Worse things happen at sea, as my grandfather used to say. I expect I'll live! Did you manage to have a look at the stuff in the folder?"

"Yes. There wasn't a lot in it, but what there was does make pretty interesting reading. Definitely quality rather than quantity!"

"Oh yes?" Carl's face brightened. "What did you find out?"

"Quite a bit, but can it wait until we get to the library? I think Mr Sykes should hear it too, and it would save having to tell it all twice."

"OK. I've waited for long enough, I can wait a few more minutes!"

"But I have managed to solve one mystery," Emily added, as Carl negotiated the car out into the traffic.

"What's that?"

"I was talking to my aunt last night about the Second World War, and I found out what happened to my grandfather – the one I never knew."

"Oh yes?"

"It seems that he was killed in a freak air raid in Somerset in 1942." She briefly repeated what Auntie May had told her. "And he hasn't even got a headstone," she ended sadly. "Gran couldn't afford one."

"That's very sad. I'm so sorry."

"Thank you." She smiled gratefully. "Oh, there's something else."

"What?"

"I remembered last night where I'd heard the phrase *Gott mit uns*. I thought it sounded vaguely familiar, but I couldn't quite put my finger on why. But it was the motto of the German Army in the First World War."

"So, is there some connection with the German Army, do you think?"

Emily nodded.

"Yes. But perhaps I ought to warn you: if I've understood it correctly, the whole thing does sound rather complicated. And I don't think we've found all the answers, even now."

***

Emily made her way into the library as Carl took the car round to the other side of the park. Brenda, already sitting at the front desk and looking through the morning post, glanced up as she approached. Karen was nowhere to be seen.

"Morning!"

"Morning. How are you getting on with Mr Sykes and his friend?"

"Quite well, thanks. I've got something I need to show them. Do you need me at the moment, or can I go straight through?" Emily gestured towards the reference section.

"No, go on. I know where you are if I need you."

"Thanks." Emily glanced round. "Where's Karen?"

Brenda frowned and lowered her voice to a whisper.

"The good Lord alone knows. And he isn't telling."

The two women exchanged worried looks; the silence between them spoke volumes.

Emily hung up her coat, switched on the photocopier and began to sort out the morning papers, arranging them in their usual places on one of the tables in the reference section. When Mr Sykes appeared a few minutes later, she already had the photocopy of that morning's crossword ready to hand to him.

"Good morning, fair lady!"

"Morning, Mr Sykes. Here you are!"

"As I told you yesterday, my name is Alf!"

Emily gave him a shy smile.

"Sorry. But somehow I can't get used to the idea of calling you by your first name."

"Why ever not?"

"I don't know. Well, perhaps I do. It's something my mum was always very particular about. She always told me that – er – older people..." She paused, as if embarrassed to continue. "Sorry. No offence intended."

"None taken, I assure you." Mr Sykes beamed in an avuncular sort of way.

"Thank you. Anyway, my mum would never let me call older people by their first names. She said it was disrespectful. She insisted that I should call them Mr or Mrs, or if they were her friends, I could call them Auntie or Uncle. As I was growing up, I got thoroughly confused about who were my real relatives and who weren't!"

"I bet you did!" Mr Sykes raised his eyebrows. "But I suppose you could always call me Uncle Alf!"

Emily was spared the need to reply by Carl appearing in the entrance of the reference library.

"How about those letters, then?"

Chapter Fourteen

The three of them settled themselves at the table and Emily picked up her bag. From it, she carefully extracted Carl's leather folder and a sheaf of papers.

"They appear to be letters from the First World War, but there are only a few of them. And they all date from just a few months in 1918."

Carl looked up eagerly.

"Who wrote them?"

"Hans – the one whose birth certificate we found yesterday."

"The one who was born in 1900?" Carl asked.

Emily nodded.

"1918, you say?" Mr Sykes asked thoughtfully. "That would figure – he would have signed up when he was eighteen."

"So what do they say?"

"Here." Emily pushed the folder across the table to Carl, then handed him the other sheaf of papers. "These are the notes I made last night. I hope they make some kind of sense."

"Thanks." Carl beamed at her, then picked up the first sheet of paper and began to read aloud:

Tuesday 23rd April, 1918

Dearest Mother and Father,
We arrived here two days ago after a long march. I cannot tell you exactly where we are but please be assured that Peter and I are both safe and well.
We have not yet moved into our proper headquarters, so the men

are currently sleeping in barns and woodsheds, but there is plenty of straw so it is not too uncomfortable. At the moment we are doing some basic training before they send us to the front line. I do not know yet when that will be but I will write again as soon as possible.

Your loving son,
Hans

Carl looked up from the paper in his hand.

"Who's Peter?"

"I'm not exactly sure," Emily answered. "But he does mention Peter in the other letters as well. It almost sounds, from what Hans has written, as though Peter might be his brother."

"Another brother?" Carl raised his eyebrows.

"Well," Mr Sykes said thoughtfully, "if Hans was born in April 1900, and your grandfather was born in December 1903, then it isn't – pardon the expression – inconceivable that there could have been another one in between."

Carl added up on his fingers.

"Or even two, at a push!" he remarked.

"Are there any more birth certificates in there?" Emily gestured towards the bag.

"I've no idea. Perhaps we'd better have a look."

Carl reached for the bag and made as if to open it, but Mr Sykes held up his hand.

"All in good time. Let's see what the rest of the letters tell us first."

***

Carl picked up the second of Emily's notes.

Thursday 2nd May, 1918

Dearest Mother and Father,

We are now back in our billets after our first spell of duty on the front line. Our headquarters are clean and simple, and it is very good to get a reasonable night's sleep at last and to have time to write to you.

We were not ordered to go over the top this time, but we spent three nights in the dugout. But sleep was almost impossible because we were bombarded constantly by the shells from the other side. I have been told that the British trenches are much worse than ours. They do not have proper shelters and their dugouts are cold, wet and muddy. The weather has been very wet, so I can only begin to imagine how much worse it must be on the other side of the line.

Peter has had a heavy cold but he is better now.

Your loving son,

Hans

Carl put down the piece of paper and shuddered.

"That sounds grim."

Mr Sykes nodded. "And this is only what he was allowed to tell them."

Carl looked up in surprise.

"What do you mean?"

"All the letters the soldiers wrote from the front line were read before they were sent on. The armies were very worried about them falling into the wrong hands."

"So would that be why he said he couldn't tell his parents where he was?"

Mr Sykes nodded again.

"Yes. But there was a lot more to it than that. The conditions in the trenches were atrocious, and the bigwigs at the top certainly didn't want the soldiers telling the people at home exactly how dreadful it was. Any letters which contained stuff which was deemed 'unsuitable' were censored. So the soldiers had to be very careful what they wrote."

"How did the letters get home?" Carl asked, intrigued.

"The armies used a system called Field Post. The letters were delivered free of charge – once they'd got past the censors, of course."

"How do you know all this?" Emily asked.

"From my father. He served in the First World War."

"Front line?"

"Yes. But he was one of the lucky ones," Mr Sykes added slowly. "He came through it." He paused for a moment, as if remembering, then added brightly, "Shall we go on?"

Carl picked up the next sheet.

Friday 24th May, 1918

Dearest Mother and Father,

I hope you will be able to read this letter as I am writing in semi-darkness, so my handwriting may be very untidy. At the moment candles are in very short supply so we are only using half of our usual quota.

Since I last wrote to you we have been back to the front line again but once again we were not ordered over the top. But I spent one night on watch duty with one of the snipers. He seems to be only a couple of years older than me but he is already very experienced with a rifle. I have been issued with a gun, but I have not had occasion to use it yet.

I miss you all. How is young Nicholas? Please give him my and Peter's love. I am trying to keep a close eye on Peter, but as I am sure you will understand it is very difficult to watch his every move.

Your loving son,

Hans

"Nicholas? That would be your grandfather, then?" Mr Sykes beamed at Carl. "And here's Peter again. It's all starting to come together. Do go on!"

Carl turned to the next sheet.

Wednesday 27th June, 1918

Dearest Mother and Father,

Thank you so very much for the parcel, which you will be pleased to know has arrived here safely. The woolly socks and the vests were greatly appreciated! Although it is summer we still find that we get very cold when we have to stand around for long periods at a time. This is particularly true in the dugouts, which remain in the shade even when the sun is shining.

The soap is most welcome too. Little luxuries like that are very difficult to obtain here. I think I will need to share it out amongst my fellow soldiers – if only to make life a little more pleasant for all of us! I am sure you will understand..!

I am glad to hear that Nicholas is doing well at school. How is his piano playing coming along? Please tell him that since we arrived here I have learned some new songs, which I will teach him when we come home.

Your loving son,
Hans

"Did your grandfather carry on playing the piano when he grew up?" Mr Sykes asked.

Carl nodded. "He was very good at it, too. It was largely due to him that I first got interested in music."

"It's interesting what Hans says about the soap, isn't it?" Emily mused. "You don't generally tend to think about little details like that."

"No mention of Peter here, I notice," Carl remarked.

"No," Emily agreed. "Not by name, anyway. But read on," she added, her voice suddenly serious.

Carl quickly glanced at her with a flicker of concern in his eyes, then cautiously turned to the next sheet.

11th August, 1918

Dear Mr and Mrs Stein,
I have to inform you that your son, Private Hans Stein, has been wounded in action. His injuries are not life-threatening and he is now recovering in hospital. He has asked me to tell you that he will write to you himself in the next few days.
Sincerely,
Oberleutnant Franz Günther von Riefendorf

Carl winced.
"What happened next?"
By way of answer, Emily indicated the final sheet on the pile. "Brace yourself. It's not an easy read."

Chapter Fifteen

15th August, 1918

> *Dearest Mother and Father,*
> *I am writing this letter from the military hospital. I understand from my commanding officer that you have already been told that I have been wounded. This is true but I am now feeling much better.*
>
> *We were ordered over the top and I was hit by a stray bullet in No Man's Land. I remember nothing after that, until I woke up here in the hospital two days later. The doctors and nurses are looking after me very well and I hope to be discharged before too long, although I have no idea when I will be fit enough to go back to front line duties.*
>
> *My commanding officer has also told me that he has already written to you to tell you about Peter. I myself only found out about Peter's fate two days ago, when the officer decided that I was strong enough to be told. He has given me Peter's belt-buckle.*
>
> *I do not know exactly what happened at the time, but I have been assured that Peter died very bravely. I am sure this is true, as despite his extreme youth he was one of the bravest and finest soldiers I have ever known, and for anyone to imagine otherwise is unthinkable. Please hold on to that thought in these dark days.*
>
> *Your loving son,*
> *Hans*

Carl sighed and laid the paper aside.

"So Peter – whoever he was – didn't make it."

"From this, I think it's fairly safe to assume," Mr Sykes said gently, "that Peter was indeed Hans' – and your grandfather's – brother."

Carl nodded slowly, then picked up the small leather box and looked thoughtfully at the object inside it.

"Well, that solves the mystery of what this is."

"I've often heard about these, but this is the first time I've seen one," Mr Sykes murmured.

Carl turned to Emily.

"Is that the lot with the letters, then?"

"No, there's one more. But I didn't need to do anything with that."

Carl looked at her quizzically as she opened the folder and turned to the letter at the back. He squinted at it for a moment, then his face cleared.

"This one's in English!"

"Didn't you know?" Emily asked.

Carl shook his head.

"No. I only looked at the top one. When I saw it was in a foreign language, I assumed that they all were. It never occurred to me to look at any of the others."

He began to read:

Abbeville
Sunday 4th December, 1921

My dearest brother,
A very happy birthday to you! And also, as we say here in France: Bonne Fête! December 6th is not only your birthday but it is also the Feast of St Nicholas. The French celebrate saints' days as well as birthdays, so in a way it's a pity that yours are the same, as you will only get one celebration rather than two. Having said that, I have yet to discover the date of my own saint's name-day!
I am so much looking forward to seeing you next week. It is such a very long time since I last saw you, and I have so much to tell you.

Please can you bring some proper English tea with you? Mireille has never tasted proper tea in her life! France is such a wonderful place to live in so many ways, but sadly, the art of making good tea is one thing which the French people have not yet managed to master!

Until next week,
With fondest love,
Henri

Carl looked up and turned to Mr Sykes.

"So you were right about why my grandfather was called Nicholas. But who's this guy Henri?"

"Good question," Emily answered. "But this letter is in the same handwriting as all the others, so logically it must be Hans. But there's—"

"It's written from Abbeville," Carl mused, across Emily's last two words. "Isn't that in north-east France? Does that suggest that he might have stayed in France after the war?"

"If he did," Mr Sykes said slowly, "that could be why he changed his name to Henri. France and Germany had been fighting on opposite sides, so it stands to reason that he wouldn't have wanted to advertise his German origins."

"And it sounds as though the rest of the family were living in England by—" Carl turned back to the letter and checked the date at the top "—1921. So that's probably the point at which they changed the name to Stone."

Mr Sykes nodded in agreement.

"That would figure. Anti-German feeling was pretty strong in Britain and France in the years just after the war. And for quite some time afterwards, too. No offence!" he added hastily, winking at Carl.

Carl grinned. "None taken!"

Mr Sykes' face grew serious again.

"Can I have another look at the other letter? The one Hans sent from the hospital?"

Carl passed it across the table. Mr Sykes read it through twice, frowning, then nodded to himself and looked up.

"Do you remember what I was saying about censorship?"

"What about it?" Carl asked.

"Listen to this: *[Peter] was one of the bravest and finest soldiers I have ever known, and for anyone to imagine otherwise is unthinkable... Please hold on to that thought in these dark days.*" He tapped the paper with his finger. "I get the impression that there's a lot more to this than meets the eye."

"Oh yes?" Carl asked, intrigued. "What makes you say that?"

"Well, Hans clearly couldn't say exactly what he thought, but why would he have written this, unless someone had – as he put it – imagined otherwise? And there had indeed been some doubt about Peter's bravery?"

Chapter Sixteen

"Sorry to interrupt, Emily, but there's a phone call for you."

Emily excused herself from the table and followed Brenda back to the desk.

"Any idea who it might be?" Emily's rarely received personal phone calls at work, so her first thought was that it might be some kind of family emergency.

"I'm not sure, but whoever it was asked for you by name."

Emily nervously picked up the receiver.

"Hello, this is Emily Fisher. How can I help you?"

The voice at the other end was friendly and cheerful.

"Miss Fisher? Hello. My name is Jacqueline Frobisher, and I'm calling from *The Courier*. I believe you called us yesterday?"

"What? Oh, yes, that's right. It was about the…"

"Yes, I know. I've got the notes in front of me. Well, I have some good news and some bad news for you. The good news is, I've found what you were looking for. The bad news…"

As Emily listened intently to what Jacqueline Frobisher had to say, she could see out of the corner of her eye that Brenda was watching her quizzically, evidently trying to work out what the mysterious caller might be telling her. Emily made sure that her face gave nothing away, except that at one point she suddenly raised her free hand towards her mouth, made a fist and bit down hard on her knuckles. Eventually, she regained her composure and lowered her hand, politely thanked the caller for her help, and replaced the receiver on its cradle.

"Well?" Brenda asked her eagerly.

Emily's face creased into a broad smile as she relayed what

Jacqueline Frobisher had said.

Once the two women had managed to stop laughing, Brenda asked, "Are you going to tell her, or shall I?"

"That's a tricky one. I suggest we toss for it."

"Toss for what?" Carl had appeared at the desk.

Emily turned to face him, her pretty face still flushed with laughter.

"Please, Carl, could you go and fetch Mr Sykes? He needs to hear this, too."

"What was all that about?" Brenda whispered, as Carl headed back into the reference library.

Emily explained how, the previous afternoon, the two men had helped her to search through the back numbers of the newspaper to try and find the reference to the book which the vicar's wife had requested. Brenda agreed that, in view of their sterling efforts, they should be in at the kill. Once Carl and Mr Sykes had returned to the desk, Brenda reached into her purse and took out a 2p coin.

"OK, here goes. Heads or tails, Emily?"

"Tails, please."

The coin spun in the air and landed with a clatter on the desk. The Queen's head stared sightlessly up at them.

Brenda shrugged resignedly. Emily, Carl and Mr Sykes all watched and listened, as the older woman reluctantly picked up the phone and dialled the telephone number of the vicarage.

"Good morning, Reverend Bennett. Is Mrs Bennett in, please?"

A brief pause followed.

"Well, could I leave a message for her, please? It's the library, about the book which she asked us to order for her." She listened again. "Yes, I know she's ordered quite a few. This one was the cookery book. Please could you tell her that—" Brenda hesitated as she caught Emily's eye. "Please could you tell her that we're very sorry, but we can't get hold of it. It seems that—" Brenda cleared her throat before continuing. "It seems that it had a very restricted print-run, and copies of it are pretty well unobtainable. So sorry. Yes, thank you very much. Goodbye."

Brenda replaced the receiver and heaved a sigh of relief.

"You coward!" Emily teased her. "Why didn't you tell him the truth?"

Brenda's face grew serious for a moment.

"Come off it, Emily. Would you have told him?"

"No, you're right," Emily agreed.

"Will someone please put us out of our misery and tell us what you two fair ladies are talking about?" Mr Sykes asked politely.

"Oh, yes, of course. Sorry." Emily turned to face them. "Carl, you found the article, didn't you? Can you remember which day's paper it was?"

Carl thought for a moment.

"Thursday's, I think."

Brenda nodded.

"And what was the date last Thursday?"

"Well, today's the eighth, so last Thursday must have been…" He closed his eyes and let out a long sigh as the truth dawned. "Holy smoke! You mean it was..?"

"Yes, that's right. An April Fool."

"And we were all well and truly taken in by it!" Brenda added.

"I notice that you didn't tell the vicar what the book was called," Mr Sykes said drily. "But that's probably just as well."

"Quite," Brenda agreed. "But then, somehow I can't imagine the vicarage dining table groaning under the weight of recipes from *The Garbage Gourmet – Five Hundred And One Recipes Using Stale, Rancid Or Rotten Food.*"

"Another example of Garbage In, Garbage Out?" Carl suggested, as the four of them burst into simultaneous peals of laughter.

Chapter Seventeen

As they returned to the reference library, Carl's eyes fell on the microfiche reader in the corner.

"So what exactly is this for?" he asked, turning to Mr Sykes.

"All in good time, young man. All in good time," Mr Sykes beamed. "First of all, let's see if we can find a birth certificate for Peter. At least now we know what sort of thing we're looking for. Have you got Hans' certificate handy?"

"I think so. It should still be in here." Carl pulled the sheaf of papers out of the carrier bag. The ones which they had identified and sorted the previous day were still lying on the top of the pile. Carl extracted Hans' birth certificate and laid it out on the table.

"So, we're looking for something like this?"

Mr Sykes nodded.

"And whilst we're at it, we can look for your grandfather's one as well. You say you've never seen it?"

"No, never. It was only when we found one of his old passports that we realised his name wasn't Stone."

"I suppose that would have been the passport he used when they came to England," Mr Sykes mused. "What name did it have on his later ones?"

"I've only seen one other, and that definitely said Stone, not Stein."

"So that suggests that the family must have officially changed the name to Stone once they got to England."

"How would they have done that, do you think?" Emily asked.

"I'm not entirely sure," Mr Sykes admitted. "Nowadays it would be done by Deed Poll, but I don't know how it would have been done back then. We may yet find out, though."

He took the remaining unsorted papers out of the bag and carefully spread them out on the table. It was then only a matter of a few minutes before two further pieces of paper, each headed *Geboorte Certificaat*, stood out from the clutter around them.

"Bingo!" Emily picked them up triumphantly. "Here we are – Nicholas, born 6th December, 1903, and Peter, born 15th February, 1902."

"1902, you say?" Carl added up on his fingers. "That would have made him sixteen in 1918."

Mr Sykes nodded.

"So he would still have been too young to sign up, but not too young to pretend he was eighteen."

"But Hans was eighteen, wasn't he?" Emily remarked. "If they signed up together, and if the authorities knew they were brothers, wouldn't they have questioned Peter's age?"

"Not necessarily," Mr Sykes answered. "The authorities might not have known they were brothers. Or even if they did know, they were probably so desperate for soldiers by that stage that I don't suppose they were too fussy about looking at the paperwork very closely. If indeed they bothered to look at it at all."

Carl remained silent for a few moments. "If Hans is still alive," he said slowly, "then he must hold the key to what happened. In which case, we need to find him."

"That," Mr Sykes said laconically, "could be tricky."

Carl sighed.

"That's putting it mildly. I don't even know where to start."

"I'm not so sure." Emily's eyes twinkled.

Carl looked up.

"What do you mean?"

Emily smiled enigmatically and picked up the leather folder

again. "Did you notice what else was in here?"

Carl shook his head, bewildered.

"Look at this." Emily opened the folder and turned to the back. "I was just about to tell you about it, but then we got sidetracked on to other things."

The inside of the folder's back cover consisted of a flat pocket, which covered about two-thirds of its surface. Emily eased her hand into the pocket and pulled out a plain white postcard.

"This might be one place to start."

On one side, the card bore a French stamp and an Abbeville postmark, and was addressed – in the same handwriting as the letters – to "Mr Nicholas Stone" at an address in Littlefield. On the other side was printed, in French, the notification that Henri and Mireille Pierre would, with effect from 7th June, 1962, be moving to a new address in St-Omer, a few miles south of Calais.

"Pierre?" asked Carl, mystified.

Emily nodded.

"Your family certainly knew their languages! When they came to England, they changed Stein to Stone. Hans – or rather, Henri – went to France and changed Stein to Pierre."

"I thought Pierre was French for Peter."

"It is, but it's also French for stone. Clever, isn't it?"

Carl raised his eyebrows thoughtfully.

"What do you suggest?" he asked after a moment.

"Try writing to this address."

"Would he still be there?"

"Goodness knows. This is dated twenty years ago, but what have you got to lose? Even if he isn't still living there, it might still find him."

"But what should I say?"

"Perhaps I can help," Mr Sykes said gently. "I've done a lot of this sort of thing over the years. Can I draft something for you?"

Carl's face lit up.

"Would you mind?"

"Not at all. We know that he speaks English, so we can write to him in English. The only problem, if he isn't still living there now, is how we can ask for it to be forwarded on to him. If whoever is living there now doesn't understand English, that could be tricky."

"I can deal with that," Emily said quietly.

"What?"

"I did French as well as German. I can write a brief covering note to go with it, if you want."

Carl stared at her in undisguised admiration. She caught his eye and her heart performed an elaborate somersault.

"Well then," she murmured, once she had found her voice again, "let's get cracking, shall we?"

***

About five minutes later, Mr Sykes laid down his pen and turned to Carl.

"How does this sound?

Dear Mr Pierre,

I am currently doing some research into my family history, and I have recently come across some information which leads me to believe that you may be related to me.

My name is Carl Stone, and I am the grandson of Nicholas Stone, who was born on 6th December, 1903 in Eindhoven, Holland. Sadly, my grandfather passed away six months ago, but I have found your details amongst his papers, and the information suggests that you may have been his elder brother.

I would be most grateful if you could contact me as soon as is convenient for you.

Yours sincerely,
Carl Stone

"I hesitate to say 'at your convenience'," Mr Sykes grinned, as he handed the paper to Carl. "I always think that sounds too much like a public toilet!"

Carl chuckled.

"That sounds fine. Thank you very much. I'll copy that out ready to send."

"Here, you'll need this, too." Emily handed him another sheet of paper, on which she had written a few sentences in French.

"What does this mean?" Carl asked.

"It just says: *Dear Sir or Madam, Please be so kind as to forward this letter to Monsieur Henri Pierre, if he is no longer living at this address. Many thanks.* That's the gist of it, anyway!"

"Thank you," Carl smiled at her again, then glanced at his watch. "It's almost one o'clock. I think we should go and reward ourselves with some lunch!" He stood up and turned to Mr Sykes. "Will you join us?"

"It's very kind of you to offer, but no thank you. I'll keep an eye on this stuff for you and have a go at the crossword."

"Are you sure?"

"Quite sure, thank you. And afterwards, when you get back, we'll have a look at that machine over there."

***

"What will you have to eat?" Carl asked, as they made their way across the road.

Emily considered. "You've tried the lasagne. Would you recommend it?"

"Well, it was certainly very good when I had it on Tuesday. So it should be fine, as long as they aren't serving the very same lasagne today."

Emily looked at him quizzically.

"What do you mean?"

Carl grinned. "It's a very old 'Waiter, waiter' joke:

105

'Waiter, this piece of cod isn't nearly as nice as the one I had here last week.'

'It should be, sir, it's off the very same fish…'

"As I said, it's an old joke. But you must admit it isn't bad for a clean one!"

Emily chuckled. It felt so good to be with someone who could make her laugh.

"Very well, then, the lasagne it is."

"Fine." Carl opened the door of the café and stood aside to let her through. "You go and find somewhere to sit down, I'll go and get it and be right with you. Would you like anything to drink?"

"Just glass of water will be fine, thanks."

Emily settled herself at the same table they had occupied the previous evening. A couple of minutes later Carl joined her, and placed two tumblers and a large bottle of chilled sparkling water on the table.

"This was today's special offer," he explained, as he sat down opposite her. "Buy a main course and get a free drink. They're going to bring the food over to us. They were just bringing a new batch out of the oven."

He carefully loosened the top of the bottle, pausing briefly as the gas escaped with a satisfying hiss, then filled up the two glasses.

"Well, here's to a successful outcome to the quest. Cheers!"

"I'll drink to that. Cheers!" Emily clinked her glass with his and took a grateful draught of the cool sharp liquid. "That goes down very well. I hadn't realised how thirsty I was."

"It's gone down very quickly, too," Carl remarked, as she set her half-empty glass down on the table. "It looks as though it's hardly touched the sides." He picked up the bottle again and replenished her glass.

"Thank you."

"No, I'm the one who should be saying thank you."

"What for?"

"For all your help with this. I couldn't have done it without you."

"Not at all. It is my job, after all."

Carl's face fell. "Oh, I see."

"What do you mean?"

He looked up and his eyes met hers.

"Sorry. I should have realised that it's your job to help people who come to the library. It's just that I'd hoped that…" His voice trailed off.

"That what?" Emily murmured. Her heart was hammering in her ears.

"Two lasagnes?"

They jumped and looked up as the waitress appeared at the side of the table. Carl smiled and nodded.

What, Emily wondered, had he been about to say? What had he hoped? She so desperately wanted to know. But *Nice Girls Don't Ask Questions Like That*, she told herself firmly.

So instead she just glanced down at the steaming plates, then picked up her fork.

"*Bon appetit!*"

Chapter Eighteen

Back in the library, Mr Sykes greeted them excitedly.

"I hope you don't mind, but I had another look through these papers whilst you were out. And look what I've found!"

He held up a single sheet of yellowing foolscap paper. It was covered in typescript and bore the letterhead of a firm of solicitors in Dover.

"What's this?" Carl asked.

"Take a look!"

The paper was headed *Statutory Declaration of Change of Name.*

"It would appear from this," Mr Sykes went on, as Carl began to read through it, "that as soon as your grandfather's family arrived on British soil, one of the first things they did was to find a solicitor and change the family name officially."

"When is it dated?" Emily asked eagerly.

Mr Sykes pointed to the bottom of the sheet. "The nineteenth of December 1918."

Carl whistled under his breath. "That's only a month after the war ended. So they didn't waste any time coming to England, did they?"

"No," Mr Sykes agreed. "But we're still no nearer to knowing why they left Holland."

"Here's hoping that Hans – or Henri – will be able to tell us," Emily remarked. "If we ever manage to find him."

"That reminds me," Carl added, "I need to post that letter to him. And I need to buy one or two provisions for the weekend. I'll be back in a jiffy." He excused himself and headed for the door.

"When you get back," Mr Sykes called after him, "we'll take a look at that machine."

"How did you get on with the crossword today?" Emily asked, as they waited for Carl to return.

"Not too badly, thanks. I've almost finished it, but there's one which has got me completely stumped. I've got all the letters towards it, but I'm beginning to wonder if there's been a misprint with the clue. Look."

Emily sighed sympathetically.

"There's no point in asking me about it. I wouldn't know where to start with a crossword. But I might be able to tell if there's a misprint. Which one is it?"

"Eighteen down." He handed her the paper and pointed at it with his pen.

"Oh. I see what you mean!"

The crossword grid was completed, as Mr Sykes had said, apart from the answer for 18 down. It was an eight-letter word, and he had filled in the letters which intersected with the clues from the words going across: – L – E – E – S. But where the clue would normally have been, there was merely a blank space, with a figure 8 in brackets at the end of it.

Emily frowned at it for a few moments, then reluctantly handed it back to him.

"Sorry, Mr Sykes. I haven't a clue."

Mr Sykes froze.

"What? Could you say that again, please?"

Mystified, Emily repeated it.

Mr Sykes' face broke into a broad grin.

"Miss Fisher, you are a genius!"

"What do you mean?"

"You just said you haven't a clue. And neither has the answer. It isn't a misprint at all. It's CLUELESS!"

Emily's jaw dropped.

"You mean I've actually helped to solve a cryptic crossword

clue? Really? I should like this day to be declared a public holiday!"

Mr Sykes grinned again.

"I must admit it's a very clever clue. Anyone who does crosswords on a regular basis generally gets to know how the individual compilers think. I've now got to the stage where I can usually tell when the paper has changed the compiler. Some of them are very fond of anagrams, for example. Others use a lot of abbreviations. But this one is completely off the wall."

"Perhaps that particular one was designed by a committee," Emily suggested. "Or maybe it was supposed to have gone in last Thursday. After all, it would have made a very good April Fool!"

***

When Carl reappeared with a carrier bag full of shopping, the three of them rearranged their chairs around the table which held one of the microfiche readers.

"So, what exactly does this do?" Carl was intrigued.

By way of answer, Mr Sykes opened one of the metal drawers. It contained a large quantity of brown cardboard boxes. He picked one out, apparently at random, and opened it. The contents were revealed to be dozens of sheets of dark blue celluloid, each about the size of a standard picture postcard.

"These," he explained, "are microfilm records of the births, marriages and deaths index for England and Wales."

"Really? Don't you have to go to somewhere in London for those?" Carl looked puzzled.

"Well, yes and no. The full registers are still held at the Central Records Office, so if you want to get hold of copies of proper birth, marriage or death certificates, you still need to apply to them directly. But this is the index – a sort of summary of the records which are held there. And if you've got the time and the patience, you can find out quite a lot just from these."

"What sort of things?" Emily asked eagerly.

"Here, let me show you."

Mr Sykes flicked through the sheets of celluloid in the box, then eventually selected one and pulled it out. He carefully inserted it between the two glass plates on the front of the microfiche reader, then pressed the switch which turned on the machine. The screen gave out an eerie, fuzzy blue light.

"Now what?" Carl watched, fascinated.

Mr Sykes twiddled a knob on the front of the machine. Suddenly the display popped into focus, and the screen was filled with columns of white typescript on a dark blue background.

"Why are they all in negative?" Emily asked.

Mr Sykes raised his eyebrows thoughtfully.

"Good question. I don't rightly know. I suppose it must be something to do with they way they were put on to the microfilm."

"So were they on paper originally?"

Mr Sykes nodded.

"I think the paper index still exists somewhere, though I imagine it takes up rather a lot of space." He glanced around. "Probably the equivalent of most of that wall over there."

Emily peered at the display. "How many pages do you get on one of those sheets?"

Mr Sykes considered. "I don't know exactly, but quite a lot. At a rough guess, I'd say about twenty or so."

"Quite a space-saver, then," Carl remarked.

"Apart from the machine which you need to be able to read them," Emily added drily.

"Now, if I've worked this out correctly," Mr Sykes went on, turning back to the display, "this one should have my own birth record on here somewhere."

"How do you know what sort of thing you're looking for?"

"First of all, you need the right type of list – birth, marriage or death. They're all listed and grouped separately. The labels are on the front of those drawers. Then you need to find the record for the right period. The records are indexed by year, then by quarter, then by surname, and finally by first name – and, if you're lucky, middle initial."

"So do you need to know the date before you start looking?" Carl asked.

"In theory, yes, but it isn't absolutely essential. As long as you've got a vague idea of the date – even to within a couple of years either side – you can do it by trial and error. Just keep searching through the lists until you find the record you're looking for. You'll still find it eventually – it just takes a bit longer, that's all."

As Mr Sykes adjusted the position of the lever on the front of the microfiche reader, Emily and Carl watched as the columns of print on the screen moved around. Each of the pages appeared to be headed *Births – Sept Qtr 1919*, and each column was headed *SYKES*.

"There seem to be a lot of people called Sykes," Carl observed.

Mr Sykes nodded.

"Yes, it's a pretty common name. This is one instance where it helps if you have a bit more information than just a surname."

"So we're looking for someone called Alfred Sykes?"

"Er, no. Not in this case," Mr Sykes replied sheepishly.

"But I thought your name was Alf?"

"It is. At least, that's what I've always been called. But Alfred is my middle name. My first name is Norman."

"So why have you always been called Alf?"

"Because my father's name was also Norman. It was a family tradition that the eldest son should always be named after his father. But, as I'm sure you can imagine, having two people called Norman Sykes living under the same roof caused no end of confusion. My mother realised this very early on. She was happy to go along with the tradition, but only on condition that I could be known by my middle name!"

"So if we'd been looking for Alfred Sykes, we'd have drawn a complete blank?"

"Yes. That's why it helps to gather as much information as you can before you start looking at the lists. Now, I was born in August 1919. As indeed," he added with a twinkle in his eye, "were rather a lot of other people. Mostly, they were people whose fathers had come home from the war nine months earlier!"

Emily and Carl both chuckled.

"So my birth would have been registered in the September quarter of 1919."

"September quarter? What does that mean?"

"For recording purposes, the year was divided into four quarters: March, June, September and December," Mr Sykes explained. "Births, marriages and deaths which took place during January, February and March were recorded in the March quarter. Correspondingly, April, May and June were the June quarter; July, August and September were the September quarter; and October, November and December were the December quarter. So to find my birth, which was in August, we'd need to look in the lists for the September quarter."

He manoeuvred the lever around, until the display was narrowed down to a list consisting entirely of *SYKES, Norman.*

"Which of these are you?" Carl asked.

"Good question. On the face of it, I could be any of them."

"So how do you know which is the right one?"

"Well, this is where the little extra knowledge comes in useful. As I said, my full name is Norman Alfred Sykes. So we can immediately eliminate all the names which have a different middle initial. That leaves us with this lot here." His finger circulated the appropriate area of the screen. "And we needn't bother with all these at the beginning of the list, either, because they don't have a middle initial at all. Which leaves us," (he pointed again) "with just these four."

"But we still don't know which one of these four people called Norman A Sykes is you," Emily remarked.

"Indeed. That's where this column here comes in."

"What's that?"

"It's the mother's maiden surname. My mother's maiden surname was Blackwood. So all we need to do now is look for the entry which has 'Blackwood' in this column, and that will eliminate all the others on the list."

"But what are these other columns?"

"These show where the birth was registered. This column here – the place name – is the registration district. In my case, that was Woolwich, East London. Where the birth was registered would be determined by where the birth actually took place. Each registration district had clearly defined boundaries."

"What, a bit like the catchment area for a school, you mean?" Emily asked.

"I hadn't thought about it in those exact terms, but yes, I suppose that's about right."

"And what about the other two columns?" Carl asked. "They're just letters and numbers. What do they mean?"

Mr Sykes pointed at the screen again.

"All the entries were made in official ledgers, and all the ledgers were individually numbered within the registration districts. So this figure here is the district volume number – Woolwich is 1d – and the last one is the page number within that volume."

"But I still don't quite understand what this list is for," Carl frowned. "In what way is it supposed to help?"

Mr Sykes thought for a moment before answering. "Well, if you want to look something up in a book, where is the first place you would look?"

"In the index, of course," Emily answered immediately.

"Exactly. And what would that tell you?"

"Whereabouts in the book you would find what you're looking for."

Mr Sykes nodded.

"Well, it's just the same with these lists. If you want to find the full record, they tell you which register, in the vast library of registers held at the records office, is the one you need to look at."

"Oh, I see," Carl nodded, after a moment. "But you said just now that these lists on their own could tell us a lot? What exactly did you mean by that?"

Mr Sykes beamed. He returned to the drawer, extracted another box, and took out another microfiche sheet.

"Well, we now know from these lists that I was born in London in 1919, and that my mother's maiden surname was Blackwood."

"Yes. So?"

"So we can now look for a record of my parents' marriage."

The Births index sheet was quickly replaced by one labelled *Marriages – Dec Qtr 1918*.

"I realise," Mr Sykes went on, as he whizzed through the lists on the screen, "that in terms of dates this one is about as straightforward as it can get. I know that my father came home in November 1918 and my parents were married only a couple of weeks later, so that very conveniently narrows down the area we need to search. And in the case of a marriage, there should be two entries – one for each surname. But it's always easier to search for the less common surname first."

"What do you mean by 'there *should* be two entries'?" Emily asked. "Have you ever come across any cases where there was only one?"

"No, not so far," Mr Sykes answered, "although I did once come across one where the bridegroom's name – it was a foreign name, if I remember rightly – was spelled differently in the two lists. And quite a lot of the marriages which took place during the Second World War show two alternative surnames for the wives."

"Why would that have been, do you think?"

Mr Sykes looked up, his eyebrows raised thoughtfully.

"I don't know for certain, but I expect that they might have been widows who were remarrying. The two surnames could have been the maiden name and the married name from the first marriage. A lot of that went on during the war, you know. The old order went right out of the window. There was a definite sense of 'seize the moment, for it may not come again.' And all too often," he added sadly, as he turned back to the screen, "it didn't."

Emily, recalling what Auntie May had told her about Alice and her soldier boyfriend, could not help but nod in silent agreement. She was grateful that Carl and Mr Sykes were both firmly focussed on the screen, and failed to spot her barely-suppressed shudder.

"Look – here we are!"

Emily's gaze followed Mr Sykes' pointing finger as he explained.

"Surname: Blackwood. First name: Elizabeth. Spouse surname: Sykes. District: Woolwich. Volume: 1d. Page: 47."

"But that doesn't tell you what the spouse's first name was, does it?" Emily observed.

"Well spotted," Mr Sykes beamed. "You're beginning to get the hang of this, aren't you? No, you're right; it doesn't. But there is a way to find out. Now, let's pretend that we don't already know that my father's first name was Norman. So the way we'd find that would be by looking for the other marriage entry – the one that's listed under Sykes rather than Blackwood."

Emily and Carl watched, fascinated, as he whizzed through another long list of marriages, all of which began with the surname Sykes. But this time, instead of looking in the column which gave the first name of the principal spouse, his finger carefully traced the entries in the column on the screen displaying the surname of the other spouse – eventually halting when he reached the name Blackwood.

"Here it is. Now, if this is the correct entry, then the district, volume and page number should all correspond exactly with the other one that we looked at just now. Woolwich, 1d, page 47. So then we check the first name of the spouse in this column here, and – bingo!"

Mr Sykes picked up a sheet of paper and wrote down: *Norman Sykes and Elizabeth Blackwood, married December Quarter 1918 in Woolwich. Index reference: Vol 1d, Page 47.*

"And we've found out all that just from these lists?" Carl whistled under his breath.

"Quite. And just by working back from my birth record. So we can apply this same principle to searching for your English ancestors. It won't help with the overseas ones, of course, but it will help to flesh out the other side of your family tree. That will keep our minds occupied whilst we're waiting for a reply from Hans."

"I had no idea about any of this," Carl said excitedly. "It's quite fascinating!"

"Though if we wanted to find out the exact date of the marriage," Mr Sykes went on, "we'd need to get hold of a copy of the actual marriage certificate. But we've now got the reference we need to make sure that we ask for the right one."

"Where would you get the certificate from?" Emily asked.

"You'd order it from the Central Records Office. Have you got a London telephone directory?"

Emily nodded, and pointed towards the opposite corner of the room.

"Over there. I think we've got them for the whole country."

"Good. The address should be in there…" He broke off. "What's the matter?"

Emily was sitting very still, staring fixedly into the middle distance.

"It's just occurred to me. You know I said the other day that my birth certificate didn't look like those you were showing us? Well, does this mean I should be able to get hold of a copy of the proper one, and find out what it should look like?"

"I don't see why not," Mr Sykes answered. "I don't think there's anything in the rule book to say that you can only apply for old ones. But first you'll need to find the record in the index, like we've just been doing. When were you born?"

"June 1956."

"Here, let me." Carl pulled open one of the other drawers and took out a box labelled *Births, 1956-57, E-G*, and held it out to Mr Sykes. "Would this be the right one?"

Mr Sykes nodded and beamed. "Yes, that's the one. See, you're learning fast!"

Emily leafed through the sheets of celluloid and eventually pulled out one headed *FIS*.

"There seem to be rather a lot of Fishers," she muttered, as she peered at the screen. "This could take some time."

"Try looking at the first name on the sheet," Carl suggested. "That should give you some idea if you're in the right area."

"Thanks. I hadn't thought of that."

But even so, it still took several attempts before Emily finally located the correct sheet.

"Have you got a middle name?" Carl asked, as she began to plough her way through the long list of Emily Fishers.

Emily nodded sheepishly. "Yes, but I'd rather not say what it is. I don't really like it."

"That doesn't matter," Mr Sykes said. "You only need the initial. What does it begin with?"

"C." She peered at the screen again. "There still seems to be rather a lot of Emily C Fishers."

"Look for your mother's maiden surname," Mr Sykes reminded her. "What was it?"

"Brookes, with an e," Emily replied, with an apologetic shrug. "Not exactly uncommon, I'm afraid."

"It could be worse," Mr Sykes grinned. "It could have been Smith, for example!"

Emily narrowed her search to the appropriate column, but

after going backwards and forwards through the list several times, she eventually looked up from the screen in bewilderment.

"I can't find it."

"What?" Carl returned her puzzled look.

"Well, there are lots of Emily C Fishers here, but not one of them has Brookes, with or without an e, as the mother's maiden surname."

"Have you looked at the ones that don't have a middle initial?" Mr Sykes suggested. "It's possible that the C might have been missed out."

Emily scrutinised the screen again.

"Might have been, but hasn't," she sighed at last. "There are no Brookeses there, either."

"There is one possible explanation," Mr Sykes said, after a moment's thought. "If I remember rightly, I think you get up to six weeks in which to register a birth. So if you were born in June, it's quite possible that your birth wasn't registered until July. In which case, it would be in the lists for the September quarter."

It was the work of only a few minutes to find the right section of the September quarter births, and feed the appropriate sheet into the microfiche reader. Emily noticed that in the meantime, Carl's chair appeared to have moved slightly closer to hers. As he settled himself into the seat, she became aware of the gentle pressure of his knee against hers under the table.

She caught her breath and turned hastily back to the screen, hoping that neither he nor Mr Sykes had noticed how her cheeks had suddenly reddened and her breathing had quickened. But, instead of instinctively recoiling and moving away – as nice girls are supposed to do – she found that the feeling was far from unpleasant. And she also found that her own knee, as if of its own accord, had begun to return the pressure...

She forced herself to concentrate on the task in hand.

"Fisher, Emily…Fisher, Emily C. Mother's maiden surname Brookes…" she muttered under her breath, as she focussed her eyes on the lists of names.

Eventually her voice trailed off and she stared fixedly at the screen.

"It isn't here either."

"What?" Mr Sykes gasped. "I don't see how…"

"Believe me, it isn't. Can you see it, Carl?"

Carl glared at the screen, as if by sheer force of will he could make the missing information appear. But eventually he shook his head reluctantly.

"No, you're right. It isn't there."

"So," Emily said slowly, "it would appear, from these records, that I don't actually exist."

Chapter Nineteen

"Are you sure you're all right?" Carl asked later, as they walked back to where he had left the car. There had been an unspoken assumption that he would give her a lift home again this evening.

"Yes, thanks. Why do you ask?"

"You seemed a bit – well, shaken."

Emily smiled. "Well, I was, to begin with. But then, as Mr Sykes said, there's probably a perfectly simple explanation. What was the phrase he used?"

"Something like 'delayed registration', I think."

"'Late registration'?"

"Yes, that was it. Sorry."

"But it might explain why I've only got that very basic birth certificate," Emily went on thoughtfully. "Though I still can't think why it wasn't registered properly at the time; my parents never mentioned it." She sighed. "And it's going to take ages to plough through all the other lists to find it. It could be anywhere."

Carl sighed and nodded.

"I'd love to come and help you look for it, but I'll be back at work next week."

"It doesn't matter. It isn't exactly a high-priority task. I was just curious about it, that's all. I expect I can look for it myself in odd moments." She sighed again. "Though I might have rather a lot of odd moments before too long."

"Have you heard any more about that?"

Emily shook her head, then forced a smile.

"But I'm not going to think about it now. I've got four whole days when I don't have to! And who knows what next week will bring?"

"What are you doing over Easter?"

"I don't know. Nothing definite. I haven't really thought about it, to be honest. How about you?"

"I'm supposed to be going to my parents' for lunch on Sunday, but other than that, no."

"Where do your parents live?"

"Wellbeck. It isn't too far to go."

Emily nodded in agreement.

"It's a nice village. It always seems so well looked after. Didn't it win the Village in Bloom award last year?"

"Yes. My mum did some of the planting for it."

"Does she like gardening, then?"

"She loves it. She looks after my garden for me, too. Just as well really, otherwise the weeds would grow so high that I'd never even get to the front door!"

Emily chuckled.

"Do you have any plans for this evening?" Carl asked conversationally, as they arrived back at the car.

Emily's heart leapt, but she forced herself to remain calm. She shook her head.

"I have arranged a heavy schedule of watching paint dry," she announced gravely.

"Are you an expert on watching paint dry?" He unlocked the car and opened the door for her.

Emily laughed.

"Well, I seem to do a fair amount of it, though I'd hardly consider myself to be a world authority on it. Why?"

Carl shrugged.

"I just wondered. It's just that my dad told me the other day that The White Lion in Wellbeck has changed hands, and it's just been refurbished and redecorated. In fact, I think it's reopening tonight. So, if your arrangements aren't set in concrete, how do you fancy casting an eye over the paint drying there, and giving me the benefit of your expert opinion?"

Oh help, Emily thought, what should I say? I really, really want to go. But if I sound too eager, what will he think? *Nice Girls Don't Do That…*

She opened her mouth to reply. What came out was a bright and enthusiastic:

"Thank you. That would be lovely. That is, if you don't mind spending your evening with someone who doesn't officially exist!"

Carl grinned as he started the engine.

"I expect I can cope. I'll pick you up about eight."

***

Emily had intended to ask Auntie May if she could shed any light on why her birth registration was missing from the index. But the prospect of spending the evening with Carl had immediately banished all other thoughts from her mind. Over the evening meal, she explained briefly to her aunt that she would be going out with a friend at about eight o'clock.

Auntie May offered no comment or opinion, apart from a brief "That's nice, love. Have a good time."

How very different, Emily thought as she went upstairs to change, from how it would have been under the old regime. With her mother, it would have involved third-degree interrogation, draconian rules and a non-negotiable curfew. She shuddered at the memory.

She washed and dried her hair, then spent the next three-quarters of an hour trying on outfit after outfit, before finally settling on a pair of plain but elegant trousers and a simple fitted blouse. By the time she was ready, it was already five-to-eight. The next five minutes were probably the longest five minutes of her life so far.

Chapter Twenty

The White Lion, a former eighteenth-century coaching inn, had been tastefully renovated but had managed to hold on to a lot of its original features. Carl and Emily made their way to the bar and ordered their drinks, then settled themselves comfortably at a small table in front of a cheerful log fire, which was blazing welcomingly in the enormous feature fireplace.

"There doesn't seem to be very much paint drying," Emily observed, glancing around. The beautiful natural stone walls – which, the new landlord explained, had previously been sacrilegiously covered in plasterboard and ghastly flock wallpaper – had now been lovingly restored to their former glory. The only paint was on the window frames and the whitewashed ceiling, the latter forming a perfect background to the heavy dark oak beams.

"Oh dear," Carl said, with a show of mock anxiety, as he expertly opened a packet of dry-roasted peanuts. "I hope you're not too disappointed. I fear I've dragged you here under false pretences."

"To be honest," Emily answered, entering fully into the charade, "I find stone rather fascinating."

"Really?" Carl asked her quietly.

She was suddenly aware that he was looking at her intently, and that he had gently placed his hand over hers as she reached across the table towards the peanuts. As on the previous occasions when their fingers had briefly touched in the café, the contact made her pulse race. But this time, neither of them moved away.

"Yes, really," she said, equally quietly, smiling up into those lovely blue eyes. "Especially when it has a capital S."

Without taking his eyes off her, Carl picked up his glass with his free hand – the left one.

"Can you manage your drink like that?" Emily asked, as she picked up her own glass.

Carl nodded. "This is one of those occasions," he grinned, "when there are definite advantages to being left-handed. Cheers!"

"Cheers!" Emily raised her glass and clinked it solemnly with his. She took a cautious sip of her drink, then set it down and drew a deep breath.

"I…I find it hard to believe that you aren't already spoken for," she began. "Assuming, of course, that you aren't?" she added, suddenly alarmed, as she tried to banish the ugly spectre of Two-Timing Tony from her mind.

Carl gave her imprisoned hand a gentle squeeze.

"No. I wouldn't be here with you now if I was! But I'm not, as you put it, 'spoken for.' I haven't been for about three months, officially. Though unofficially, I suppose it's been a lot longer than that."

"What happened?" Emily took another sip of her drink. "But if you don't want to talk about it, I'd quite understand."

"No, I don't mind talking about it, but there isn't really very much to tell. Her name was Lorna. We'd been seeing each other, off and on, for about a year, but latterly it had become just a habit. We had very little in common – she hated music, for one thing! Deep down we both knew that it wasn't going anywhere, but neither of us could pluck up the courage to end it. Then she was offered a new job overseas, which gave us the excuse we needed to call it a day. To be perfectly honest, it was a blessed relief for both of us. So we just said goodbye and went our separate ways."

Emily smiled wistfully.

"It must be good to be able to part without any sort of

acrimony."

"What do you mean?" Carl looked at her steadily.

Emily hesitated.

"That boyfriend I was telling you about – his name was Ben – he…" She broke off and stared into her drink. How much should she tell him?

No, now was definitely not the time to start dissecting old wounds.

"We had a blazing row when he left," she added lamely.

"Do you regret it?" If Carl had noticed her sudden change of direction, he evidently had sufficient tact not to pursue the point.

"The row, or the split?" Emily clutched at the lifeline he had thrown her.

"Either."

Emily considered. "I regretted the row – at the time, at least – because I hate leaving anything on a sour note. But I don't regret the split. I realise now that it would never have worked out." She paused for a moment before adding, choosing her words very carefully, "We wanted completely different things."

"That sounds very like how it was with me and Lorna." Carl sighed sympathetically. "We were poles apart."

"Lorna went overseas, you said? Where did she go?"

"New Zealand. About as far away as you can go before you start to come back again! So now, I suppose," he added with a wink, "we're pretty well poles apart geographically as well. Which suits me just fine!"

Emily chuckled.

"I was afraid for a moment that you were going to say she'd gone to Argentina. Not that I have anything against the country, but I can't imagine it being a very comfortable place for British people right now, the way things are at the moment with the Falklands."

"I hadn't thought of that, but yes, I expect it's pretty grim for… Oh! Of course!"

"What?"

"That would be why my great-grandparents would have been so keen to change their surname when they came to England. And probably why Hans changed his name if he decided to stay in France. So soon after the war, they wouldn't have wanted anyone to know, or even suspect, that they'd come from Germany."

"But they hadn't, had they? Well, not directly, anyway. They'd been in Holland since 1900."

"True, but their name still sounded German. And don't forget, Hans and Peter had both fought for the German army. The family wouldn't have wanted news of that to have got out, would they? Whereas Stone – well, I don't think you can get much more English-sounding than that. I'd certainly never thought of the family as being anything other than English – born, bred and buttered."

"But why did they come to England?" Emily mused. "If they were happy in Holland, why didn't they stay there? And if they weren't, then why didn't they just go back to Germany?"

"And why didn't my grandfather ever mention it?" Carl sighed and shook his head. "And now it's too late to ask him," he added sadly.

"All the more reason why we need to find Hans."

It was only after the words were out that she realised that "you" had suddenly become "we." Until now, this had been Carl's quest, and she had been no more than a helper. But now, she knew that success in this venture was going to mean just as much to her as it already did to him.

Carl nodded.

"I wonder if we'll ever get a reply to that letter," he murmured, taking another sip of his drink. It was not lost on Emily that he, too, was referring to it as their search, rather than his. And whatever Nice Girls were or were not supposed to do, it would be churlish to let him down now, wouldn't it?

She smiled up into those lovely clear blue eyes.

"I hope so. But in the meantime, we'll just have to wait and see."

***

Emily released her seat-belt and reached down to retrieve her handbag from the footwell. Straightening up, she sensed rather than saw Carl moving towards her, his arm stretched out along the back of her seat.

She turned to face him and smiled, her eyes now on a level with his.

"Thank you for a lovely evening."

"My pleasure." He smiled through the darkness. "Thank you, too."

She could feel the warmth of his breath on her face. His hand had somehow found its way into her hair, and was gently drawing her head towards his own. The fingers of his other hand – those fingers which could take up any instrument and caress it into life – tenderly stroked her cheek as his lips approached hers. Even if she had wanted to resist, she had no time to think that Nice Girls weren't supposed to kiss on a first date.

The first tentative contact instantly lit the touch paper; every fibre of her body crackled and sparked as she eagerly surrendered her lips to his. For the first time in her life, this felt right. This felt natural. This must be how it was supposed to feel...

His lips withdrew from hers just far enough to allow him to speak. His voice was like warm honey on a cold morning.

"Can I see you again?"

"Oh yes, please!"

"Tomorrow? We could go out for the day if you like."

"That would be lovely," she answered happily.

"Fine. Shall I pick you up about half past ten?"

Emily nodded enthusiastically. Carl's lips lightly brushed hers once more. Reluctantly, she fumbled for the handle to let herself out of the car. As the door clicked open, she instinctively turned back towards him and spontaneously returned the kiss.

It was only after he had driven off into the night that it occurred to her to wonder if perhaps she might, once again, have seemed a little too eager…

***

"Is that you, love? I'm in the kitchen."

Auntie May was bustling around in her dressing gown, waiting for the kettle to boil.

"Cup of tea, love? I'm just about to make one."

"Yes, please, that would be lovely. Thanks."

"Did you have a nice evening?"

"Yes thanks." Emily hesitated, then added lamely, "We went to the White Lion in Wellbeck. It's just been redecorated."

"Who was it you went with? Someone from work, you said?"

"Well, yes and no. His name's Carl." Emily felt her cheeks burning. She was glad that Auntie May, busy counting out three teabags into the teapot, was facing away from her and couldn't see her embarrassment. "He's one of the people from the library I was telling you about. The ones who've been researching family history."

"Oh yes, love. I remember you telling me."

"I've been helping him a bit. I think this was just a way of saying thank you."

Get a grip, she told herself. You might have had to say this to justify it to your mum, but there's no need for it with Auntie May. As she's told you herself, you're a big girl now.

"Has he found out much?" Auntie May was asking, as she poured the boiling water into the teapot.

"Quite a bit, but he's waiting now to hear from someone he's written to. Oh, that reminds me. There's something I've been meaning to ask you."

"What's that, love?"

"I…"

Emily hesitated. Suddenly the question seemed to have stuck in her throat.

"What's the matter, love? Come on, spit it out."

Emily drew a deep breath. The words, once they began, came tumbling out in one long continuous torrent.

"Well, Carl had some old birth certificates, and when we were looking at them, I noticed that they have a lot more information on them than mine does. Names of parents, exact place of birth, that sort of thing. But mine just has my name, my date of birth and my country of birth – nothing else at all.

"Anyway, I've just found out how I can get hold of a copy of the whole thing. I can order it from the Central Records Office, but I need to find the index number first. We've got the indexes in the library at the moment so I had a look. But when I came to look for it, it wasn't there. There are plenty of people called Emily Fisher, but not one of them is me. And I just wondered if you knew anything about it; any reason why it might not be on the list. Like, was my birth registered late, or something like that?"

She paused to catch her breath. But Auntie May didn't reply. She was standing, as if paralysed, staring down at the worktop. When her aunt finally looked up, Emily saw that her face was deathly pale. Her eyes, as they met Emily's, betrayed a look of undisguised panic.

"What is it, Auntie May? Are you all right?"

Auntie May steadied herself against the worktop and gradually recovered her composure. Why, Emily wondered incongruously, did her aunt suddenly throw two more teabags into the pot? Surely the tea didn't need to be THAT strong. Did it?

"Yes, love, I'm all right." She drew a deep breath and set the tea-tray down on the table. "But you'd better sit down. There's something I need to tell you…"

130

Chapter Twenty-One

Carl made himself a pot of tea and sat down at his kitchen table as he waited for it to brew.

A slow smile spread over his handsome face as he thought back over the past couple of hours. What lovely company she was – and she clearly enjoyed being with him. That much had been obvious even before they had kissed. He had been afraid to make the first move, for fear of scaring her – but in the end it had all happened so naturally, without either of them even having to think about it. And it had clearly meant as much to her as it did to him.

What had taken him really by surprise was his own response. With her warm, sweet breath on his face and her warm, soft lips fusing with his own, he felt as though he had finally come home.

He had never felt even remotely like that with Lorna.

But he still had a niggling feeling that there was something Emily wasn't telling him. And now, he was more convinced than ever that it had something to do with this mysterious ex-boyfriend, Ben. Yet she had readily told him – in a bald, almost matter-of-fact way – about the tragedy which had claimed the lives of both her parents. So what could possibly have happened with this guy Ben, if it had been so traumatic at the time that she couldn't bring herself to talk about it even now?

As he reached for the teapot, his eye fell on the letter. It was still lying, defiantly, on the table where he had left it the previous evening.

You're a fine one to talk, it said to him. *Whatever it is that she isn't telling you, I bet it's nothing compared to what you aren't telling her. And anyway, her problem lies in the past. But I'm very much in the present. And the future. You can't go on ignoring me.*

He picked up the letter and read it again. Yes, you're right, he answered mentally, as he threw it back on to the table. I'm not being fair to her. And I can't keep you a secret for ever...

***

"Do you remember, love, what I told you about your mum and Tom, the soldier?"

Emily nodded.

"The one who went to India? What about it?"

Auntie May passed a mug of steaming dark brown liquid across the table. As Emily raised the mug towards her lips and its sickly sweet aroma hit her nostrils, she suddenly felt an overwhelming sense of foreboding. She carefully set the mug down on the table without tasting its contents.

"Tom and your mum loved each other to distraction..."

"Really?" Emily murmured.

"Really." Auntie May paused, then managed a wry smile. "Does that surprise you?"

"Well, yes, it does. Somehow I can never imagine Mum ever being...er..." Emily's voice trailed off as she struggled to find the right word.

"Passionate?" Auntie May suggested gently.

"Yes, that. She always seemed so calm, so reserved."

"She was, latterly," Auntie May agreed. "She was certainly like that for all the time that you knew her. But she hadn't always been like that."

"What do you mean? What happened?" Emily clenched her hands around the mug of tea. She was grateful for its warmth, although she still could not bring herself to drink any of it. But the uneasy feeling was growing that before long, and for the second time in little more than twenty-four hours, she would need to take a long, strong draught of Uncle Bert's cure for shock.

Auntie May drew a deep breath before continuing. The tale, whatever it was, was evidently very painful in the telling.

"In 1943, shortly after Tom was sent away to India," she said at last, "Alice found that she was pregnant."

Chapter Twenty-Two

Emily eventually found her voice, though when her words came out, that voice sounded nothing like her own.

"But...that couldn't have been me, could it? 1943, you said? That was more than ten years too early for it to have been me."

"No, love, it wasn't you."

"So what happened? And what did Gran say about it? I can't imagine her being too thrilled. Any more than I can imagine Mum being over the moon if it had ever happened to me," she added, half to herself.

"I don't think Gran ever knew. Your mum was very keen to make sure that she never found out. Gran had very particular views about that sort of thing."

"What sort of views?"

"Gran always maintained that an unmarried mother only had herself to blame. She said that any unwanted pregnancy was automatically the woman's fault."

"But why?" Emily winced.

"Because," Auntie May said laconically, "it was always the woman who had the final say on whether or not she kept her legs together."

Emily gasped. She would never have had this kind of frankness from Alice. Her hands tightened further around her mug.

"And, of course, nice girls didn't do that sort of thing," Auntie May went on. "Or at least, they didn't do it willingly. I think it was because your mum *had* done it willingly that she felt she couldn't face Gran."

Emily's eyes widened. "But surely Gran must have been able to tell? I mean, it isn't exactly easy to hide, is it? At least, not towards the end."

"I'm not so sure. Your mum carried on working on the farm, don't forget. Those dungarees that the girls wore in the Land Army were pretty shapeless things at the best of times, so it wouldn't have been difficult for her to keep a bulge hidden – at least for a while. Later on, when she couldn't hide it any longer, she just stayed in Somerset, well away from the rest of us, until it was all over."

Emily picked up her mug and took a grateful sip of the hot, strong, sweet liquid.

"So, she went ahead and had the baby?" she asked, finally plucking up the courage to break the silence.

Auntie May nodded.

"What happened?"

"It was a little girl, although I never saw her. She was given up for adoption as soon as she was born."

"Poor Mum…" Emily felt an involuntary tear trickling down her cheek. She wiped it away with the back of her hand, then took another longer draught of the tea. "But I don't understand. *Nice Girls Don't Do That Sort Of Thing.* That's what she was always – and I do mean always – saying to me. So why..?"

"Probably because she knew what dreadful heartache it could bring. And she was trying to save you from the same fate that she'd suffered. Though, having said that, I'm not convinced that she always went about it the right way."

"What do you mean?"

Auntie May sighed. "She was far, far too protective of you."

Emily looked up. "You could tell that?"

"Oh yes. There were lots of things that she wouldn't let you do; things which Ruth did as a matter of course. Going to parties or discos, for instance."

"I've often wondered why Ruth always seemed to have a lot more freedom than I ever did," Emily murmured, with a wry smile. "But Mum was quite subtle about it. She did let me go to the youth club, but then, that was run by the church, so I suppose that made it 'respectable'." Emily made invisible inverted commas in the air with her fingers as she spoke. "But that was the limit of it. She never actually said 'You can't go to that party.' Probably because she knew I would have asked why not, and she wouldn't have been able to give me a plausible reason. She'd say things like 'You don't want to go to that party, do you? It's not your sort of thing, is it?' – clearly expecting me to say 'No.' I did sometimes wonder what would have happened if I'd said 'Yes, I do want to go.' But on the whole, it was much easier just to go along with her and keep the peace."

"Oh, you poor thing!" Auntie May reached out and gripped Emily's hand. "I suppose that's one reason why, since you came to live with us, I've tried not to be too restrictive of what you do. So long as you've stayed within the law, of course!"

"Thanks!" Emily squeezed her aunt's hand gratefully. "But I suppose that must mean…" she paused as the realisation hit her. "That must mean I've got a sister out there somewhere!"

Auntie May's hand tightened round her own. Glancing down, Emily could see that the older woman's knuckles had turned ghostly white.

"Well, yes, love, you have," she murmured, almost inaudibly. "But it's a bit more complicated than that…"

Emily waited. Eventually Auntie May drew a deep breath.

"Your mum never really got over it. She'd lost her man and she'd lost her child in one fell swoop. When she met your dad, we were all pleased that at last she seemed to be putting the past behind her. And, of course, she was desperate to replace the child she'd had to give away. But, try as they might, they never managed to have one of their own."

Auntie May paused.

"But…" Emily stopped. The stark truth was now staring her in the face. "Where did I come from? Was I..?"

"Yes, that's right, love. They adopted you."

"So, who is my mother?"

But even before she had finished asking the question, Emily realised, as she stared across the table, that she already knew the answer.

Chapter Twenty-Three

"Please, love, can you ever forgive me?" The older woman stared at the younger one through brimming eyes.

"I don't understand. What is there to forgive?"

"I never wanted to give you away. But Alice was so determined..."

"I can well imagine that," Emily sighed. "I know only too well what she was like when she was dead set on something." She hesitated. "Please, can you tell me what happened? Though, if it's too painful..."

"No, love, you have a right to know. Alice never intended to keep it from you. She was going to tell you when you were eighteen."

Emily gripped Auntie May's hand and waited for her to speak again.

"As I said, Alice and Walter never managed to have any children of their own. I've no idea why not. It wasn't the sort of question I ever felt I could ask her."

"No, it wouldn't be." Emily nodded in agreement.

"Well, Bert and I already had Graham and Ruth, and we thought that would be it. Then, nearly five years later, we discovered that you were on the way."

"Was I an accident, then?"

Auntie May smiled. "I wouldn't say you were an accident, love, but you were certainly a surprise! Anyway, when I first mentioned it to Alice, she said something like, 'Oh, perhaps I can have this one!' At first, I thought she was joking, then it gradually dawned on me that she was deadly serious."

Emily stared.

"What about Uncle Bert?" she asked eventually. "Didn't he get any say in the matter?"

Auntie May shook her head.

"We never ever wanted to give you up – please believe that, love. But as time went on, Alice took complete control. She organised all the adoption papers, and she even wore a maternity dress for the last few months, to make the whole thing look convincing."

"How ironic." Emily hadn't intended to interrupt, but the words slipped out of their own accord. "She had to hide a real pregnancy, and then fake a false one."

"Quite. That wasn't lost on me, either." Auntie May nodded sadly. "But once Uncle Bert and I realised that it was inevitable, we tried to convince ourselves that we weren't really giving you up. After all, it wouldn't be the sort of adoption where we'd have to hand you over to total strangers then spend the rest of our lives wondering what had happened to you. We'd still be able to see you. We'd still be able to watch you grow up, and still be able to have fun with you. And we'd be giving Alice the one thing she'd always wanted. The two things we wouldn't be able to do would be to bring you up as our own, the way we would have wanted. Or hear you call us Mum and Dad…"

The last word was lost in a choked sob.

"So, when you said just now that I've got a sister…"

"Yes, love. And a brother, too. Graham and Ruth."

***

Emily stood up, walked round to the other side of the table, and took the older woman in her arms.

"Why didn't you tell me all this yourself?" she asked gently. Her voice held no hint of accusation.

"I wanted to, love. I really, really wanted to. But coming straight after the accident, I knew that it would be too much for you to cope with. Then, when you did turn eighteen, you were in the middle of doing your A-levels. I don't think you'd have thanked me for springing it on you then!"

Emily shook her head wistfully.

"No, I guess not."

"Then, the longer I left it, the harder it became. But please believe me, love, I never ever intended to keep it from you. This isn't how I'd imagined telling you, but…"

"Never mind that. You've told me now."

"You're not angry with me?"

"Angry with you? Not a bit. How can I possibly be angry with you, after everything you've been through?" Emily shuddered. "I can only begin to imagine what it must have been like for you, being bullied into giving your baby away and then having to go on pretending for all those years." She paused. "Do Graham and Ruth know?"

Auntie May shook her head. "No, love. As far as they're concerned, you're their cousin. I wanted to tell them the truth, but I couldn't tell them without telling you as well, and I wasn't sure they'd understand. And anyway, they might have accidentally let it slip. No, the fewer people who knew, the better."

"Are you going to tell them now?"

"Only if you want me to, love."

Emily considered. "I've always been an only child. It would be good to have a brother and a sister at last. But if you like, I'll make sure I'm there when you do tell them."

Auntie May fished a handkerchief out of the pocket of her dressing-gown and wiped away the tears from her cheeks.

"Thanks, love. That would be good. They're coming for lunch on Sunday. We can tell them then, if you like."

Emily nodded. "And what about you?"

"What about me?" Auntie May frowned.

"What would you like me to call you now?"

The frown dissolved into a watery smile.

"I don't really mind, love. You can call me whatever you like – as long as it isn't something rude!"

"But this still doesn't explain," Emily added after a moment, "why my birth wasn't on that list."

"Oh, I think I can explain that. But first I need to show you something. Wait here, love."

Auntie May got up from the table and went out into the hall. She returned a few minutes later, carrying what appeared to be an old biscuit tin. Its contents were revealed to be a collection of pieces of folded paper.

"Here."

She unfolded one of them and handed it to Emily. It was about fifteen inches long and just over six inches high, and was pink and cream with red printed lettering. At first glance, it looked very like one of the birth certificates which she had seen in Carl's collection of papers. But closer examination revealed that some of the column headings were subtly different. The columns on the left contained Emily's name and date of birth, but the two columns in the centre of the sheet were headed *Name and surname, address and occupation of adopter or adopters,* and *Date of adoption order and description of court by which made.*

The contents of the first column consisted of the names Walter David Fisher and Alice Elizabeth Fisher, plus the address of the house where Emily remembered spending the first few years of her life. In the second column was the name of the local county court and a date towards the end of 1956. The entries were handwritten, in the same copperplate script which Emily recalled having seen on her own simple birth certificate – presumably issued at the same time. At the bottom of the paper were printed the words *CERTIFIED to be a true copy of an entry in the Adopted Children Register.*

Emily peered at the paper and frowned. "Sorry, but I still don't understand. This still doesn't explain why I couldn't find my birth on that list."

"No, it wouldn't, love. That's because, after you were formally adopted, you were issued with a new birth certificate in your new name – Fisher. But when your birth was registered, that had to be done under your original name – our surname."

"So if I look for Emily Harrison, I should find it?"

"Well, no, not quite. Harrison, yes, but not Emily. We called you Rosemary."

"Rosemary?" Emily gasped.

Auntie May nodded.

"We'd hoped that it would stay the same after the adoption," she added sadly, "but Alice had her own views on that…" She broke off. "What's the matter, love? You've gone as white as a sheet."

"I was just…thinking… It feels really weird to think that I started out as someone else. And with a completely different name, too. Rosemary Harrison…" She gazed down into her mug of now barely tepid tea. "What happened to my original birth certificate? Have you still got it?"

Auntie May shook her head. "No, love. We had to send it back with the adoption papers. I've no idea what happened to it after that."

Emily stared down at the table. She suddenly felt unutterably weary.

"Sorry, love. Are you all right? I know this must have been a bit of a shock for you…"

"That's putting it mildly!" Emily managed a wan smile. "I'm okay, thanks. Or rather, I will be when I've had time to take it all in." She stifled an involuntary yawn. Glancing at her watch, she was amazed to notice that it was already well after midnight.

"Sorry. I've suddenly come over very tired. Do you mind if I turn in?"

"No, love, not at all." Auntie May stood up and began to clear away the tea things.

"Tell me a bit about this young man – Carl, you said his name was?"

Emily smiled. "There isn't much to tell, really. He's a musician, and he drives a Volkswagen Golf. He's very nice, very polite, and very well-spoken. He lives just outside Medford, and his parents live in Wellbeck. And we've arranged to go out for the day tomorrow."

Auntie May smiled. "That's nice, love. What time will you be going out?"

"He's supposed to be picking me up about half past ten."

"OK. I'll bring you a cup of tea about nine."

***

Emily peeled off her clothes, wiped off her make-up and brushed her teeth, then dragged her weary limbs gratefully into bed. But despite her aching fatigue, sleep would not come. She lay for a long time staring through the darkness at the shadows on the ceiling, as the maelstrom of the past couple of hours rampaged through her thoughts.

So much to take in…

The more she thought about Auntie May's revelation, the more she realised that it didn't really surprise her. Suddenly, everything had fallen into place. She had always felt more at home with May than with Alice – and she had even wondered, from time to time, why she appeared to bear much more of a family resemblance to Uncle Bert than to either half of the couple whom she had always called Mum and Dad.

And Alice? Poor, heartbroken, tragic, well-meaning Alice…

"Oh, Mum," she whispered, "I'm so very, very sorry. I hope you can hear me. I'm sorry I misunderstood you. I thought… I thought… Oh, I don't know what I thought. But now I understand. I see now that you were only trying to save me from what you went through…"

And at last, the tears came. Tears which carried away years and years of pent-up tension and frustration…

"Don't cry, love. You'll make yourself ill."

Emily caught her breath. She had heard the words in her mind as clearly as if Alice had been beside her in the room.

"What?"

"And you'll look dreadful in the morning," the voice went on. "You'll want to look your best for that nice young man of yours tomorrow, won't you?"

"Yes," Emily whispered into the darkness.

"Sleep well, love…" The voice faded.

"Thank you, Mum… Thank you for everything…"

Was this, Emily wondered, what is really meant by being haunted? Perhaps there is no need for phantoms, or apparitions, or ghostly presences. Is it simply that when you've known someone so well, and for so long, you know exactly what they would say, under any circumstances, even years after they've gone?

And for the first time since Alice's death, Emily realised that haunting need not necessarily be bad. Yes, Alice had cared about her. And even from whatever dimension lay beyond this earthly life, she still cared – enough to want Emily to be happy with "that nice young man."

Emily shuddered. Once again, Britain was at war. Might Carl be sent away to a distant continent, just as Tom had been, almost forty years earlier?

What was it that Mr Sykes had said about wartime romances?

"Seize the moment, for it may not come again."

Chapter Twenty-Four

Auntie May stepped forward with a warm smile and extended her hand. "Hello, you must be Carl. I'm May. Lovely to meet you."

"How do you do? Lovely to meet you, too." Carl shook hands and returned the smile. He turned to Emily.

"Are you ready?"

"Yes, thanks, whenever you are."

"Have a nice day, you two. Any idea what time you might be back?"

"Er…" Emily hesitated. "I hadn't really thought about that!" She turned to Carl. "Where are we going?"

Carl beamed. "Do you fancy going across to the coast?"

"That would be lovely." Emily nodded happily.

"In that case," Carl turned to Auntie May, "I should think we'll get something to eat whilst we're out. We should be back during the evening. Is that okay?"

"Yes, that's fine. Have a good time!"

Emily hugged Auntie May, then led the way to the door. As she opened it to allow Carl to go out ahead of her, she turned back and gave the older woman a grateful smile. By taking matters into her own hands and introducing herself simply as "May", she had neatly rescued Emily from the necessity of having to explain precisely who she was. For the moment, at least.

***

"Which sea area is this?" Carl asked, as they leaned on the rail at the side of the pier and stared out across the beach below.

"Either Thames or Dover, I'm not quite sure which," Emily answered, taking in deep breaths of the fresh salty air. "Ah, that's good. It certainly blows the cobwebs away. And the spiders, too, come to that!"

"And what are those birds over there?" Carl pointed to a group of black and white birds foraging in the shallows on the edge of the water.

Emily peered at them for a moment.

"Have they got long orange beaks?"

"Yes, I think so."

"In that case, I think they're oystercatchers."

"Do you get oysters around here?" Carl asked, surprised.

Emily chuckled. "I'm not sure. I don't know why they're called oystercatchers – I think they eat cockles. That's probably what they're looking for now. They use their beaks to prise the shells open, then they eat what's inside and leave the empty shells on the beach. If you ever find a cockle shell with the two halves still attached, that's usually what's happened to it."

A small dog scampered along the beach, causing the birds to screech and take off in alarm. They flew in perfect formation, their black and white plumage reflecting the spring sunshine.

"Yes," Emily nodded as she watched. "Those are definitely oystercatchers!"

Carl did not reply. Instead, he laid his hand over hers as it rested on the pier railing.

"Emily," he began gently, "there's something I have to tell you."

She turned to look at him, her face as serious as his had suddenly become.

"I've got something to tell you, too."

"What is it?"

"No, you go first."

"No, you. Ladies first!"

"OK then." She gripped his hand, as if to draw courage from its warm strength.

"I...I..."

"What is it?" he whispered. "Is it really as bad as that?"

"No." She managed a soft laugh. Somehow his light-hearted remark had broken the ice for her. The words were no longer sticking in her throat.

"I know what was wrong with my birth certificate. And why my birth wasn't on those lists."

"Oh yes?" The excitement in Carl's voice was almost tangible, but out of the corner of her eye, Emily could see his face freeze as he caught sight of the pain in her eyes.

"Sorry," he murmured. "Go on."

"The reason why it doesn't look like any of those which you had, and why it isn't on that list, is that it isn't really my birth certificate at all."

"What?" Carl gasped.

She gripped his hand again, then drew a deep breath.

"I've just found out that I was adopted. The people I'd always thought were my parents were in fact my aunt and uncle. And my aunt and uncle – the ones I've been living with since I was seventeen – are really my parents. That lady that you met this morning, who introduced herself as May, is really my mother. And the two people that I thought were my cousins are really my brother and sister..."

She paused to draw breath. Carl stared at her, open-mouthed.

"And there's something else," she went on. "I'm not really Emily Fisher. That's why I couldn't find my name on that list. My real name – the name my birth was registered under – is Rosemary Harrison. It was only changed to Emily Fisher after I was adopted." She glanced back at the birds on the beach. "It seems that they're not the only ones with the wrong name."

Without letting go of her hand, Carl put his free arm around her and gently drew her closer to him. She gratefully hid her

147

face against his shoulder as he lightly kissed the top of her head.

"Don't worry," she heard him murmur into her hair. "What's in a name? You're still the same person underneath."

"Really?" She kept her face hidden, fighting back the tears.

"Really. That which we call a rose – or, in this case, Rosemary – by any other name would smell as sweet… So Rosemary would, were she not Rosemary called…"

Emily looked up, amazed.

"What?"

Carl grinned. "I did *Romeo & Juliet* for O-level."

"Aren't you lucky?" Emily managed a watery smile. "I got *Julius Caesar* when I did it."

"I think I would have preferred that! I thought *Romeo & Juliet* was a load of soppy nonsense at the time; apart from the fighting, that is. But I've never forgotten the quotations we had to learn. And I'm sure if I'd come to it for the first time now, I would have appreciated it a lot more." He squeezed her hand again. "Old Will certainly knew a thing or two about human nature."

"I think that's true of Shakespeare in general. All too often, people are put off him because of having the stuff rammed down their throats before they're old enough to understand it." Emily smiled again, this time with a little more animation. "We see quite a lot of that at the library, with schoolchildren coming in looking for books to decode what they've been set at school. Oh, I'm sorry. Here I am, rambling on about nothing. You said you had something to tell me as well?"

Carl leaned forward and kissed her lightly on the forehead.

"It doesn't matter now. It will keep. Let's go and find some lunch."

***

"So, what was it you wanted to tell me?" Emily asked, as they sipped their post-lunch coffee.

Carl hesitated, then answered, "A few weeks ago, before I met you, I applied for a new job. My boss had told me about it. He said that if ever a job description had my name at the top, this was it. When I looked into it, I saw he was right. I knew they'd be flooded with applications so I never thought I stood a chance with it, but he insisted that I should try for it anyway."

"What sort of job?"

"It's with a group. They want someone who can do vocals and play keyboard and bass guitar, and also oversee some of the recording and mixing side of things."

"Wow, that sounds right up your street!"

Carl nodded.

"It is."

"Well? What about it?"

"I've just had a letter telling me I've got it."

"But that's wonderful! You must be thrilled."

"Well, yes, but…"

"But what?"

"That's the problem. The group does tours, so it would involve a lot of travelling, and in any case, it isn't based round here. If I take it, I'll have to move up to London."

Emily froze. Wasn't this precisely what had happened with his relationship with Lorna, when the offer of a new job had provided a much-needed excuse to end it?

"What's the matter?"

She was suddenly aware that he was speaking again.

"You'd have to move up to London?" she repeated, as she turned to face him. The words, as she heard herself saying them, sounded bald and superfluous.

Carl nodded. There was a strange sadness in his eyes – something which she couldn't quite identify.

"I knew that when I applied for it, of course, and at the time it didn't matter. But since then, I've met you, and that puts a rather different complexion on it."

"What do you mean?"

Carl drew a deep breath. "I don't want to leave you."

It seemed to Emily as though time had stopped. What on earth was she to say? He was now saying that he wanted to be with her. But if this new job really was the key to the career that he had always dreamed of, then who was she to hold him back?

She shuddered. If he turned it down because of her, and his career never progressed any further, would she ever forgive herself? Or – worse still – would he always hold it against her?

She turned her brimming eyes to his.

"Please, Carl, don't feel you have to spend the rest of your life languishing in a backwater on my account. If you want the job, you must take it. This is everything you've always wanted. Please don't sacrifice it just for me... When do you need to decide?"

"Ideally, as soon as possible. But in any case, I won't be able to do anything about it until I go back to work on Tuesday, so I've got until then to think it over..."

Chapter Twenty-Five

The following Tuesday, when Carl had gone back to work, life at the library slowly began to return to normal. Emily forced herself to try not to think about what might be happening at the studio.

Mr Sykes appeared at his usual time and took up his old routine with the crossword, though he also spent a fair amount of time trawling through the microfiches.

"I've still got some family history research of my own underway," he explained with a wink. "So I may as well use these whilst we've got them here!"

Emily managed a professional smile. "I'll leave you to it, then."

She made her way into the staff kitchen to make some coffee. As she pushed the door open, a ghastly sight met her eyes. Karen was slumped over the worktop, holding her head in her hands.

"Karen? What's the matter? Can I help?"

At the sound of the sympathetic voice, Karen appeared to lose all pretence at composure. She looked up at Emily with brimming eyes.

"Oh, Emily…" Her voice was choked with sobs. Emily reached into her pocket and passed her a tissue.

"I'm going to lose my job…"

"How do you know?" Emily asked, shocked. "Have they told you?"

Karen nodded miserably.

"I got the letter last week, but I couldn't tell anyone here until I'd told my husband. He's away, you see, and I didn't manage to speak to him until over the weekend."

"Where is he?" Emily asked, simply for the sake of having something to say. "What does he do that's kept him away over Easter?"

"He's a soldier. He's away in the Falklands."

Emily gasped. "Oh, Karen, I'm so sorry. I had no idea."

"I'm sorry, too," Karen sniffed.

"Sorry for what?"

"For letting you and Brenda go on worrying about your own jobs for all that time. I just couldn't face anyone. That's why I kept hiding from you." She sobbed again.

Emily put her arms round her.

"I don't understand, Karen. Why you? You're a good worker. I don't see why they would want to get rid of you."

Karen dabbed at her eyes.

"The letter said it was nothing to do with my work. They just said that they have to get rid of one member of staff from here. But as soon as they first made the announcement about the cutbacks, I knew I'd be the obvious choice."

"Why? What makes you say that?"

"It's how they calculate the redundancy payment. Or rather, in my case, the lack of it," Karen answered bitterly. "The longer you've worked, the more they have to pay you – so the last one in is always the first one out. But I've only been here for six months, so I wouldn't qualify for it in any case."

"Oh, Karen, you poor thing. I wish there was something I could do to help." Emily hugged her colleague as the other woman continued to sob on her shoulder. "How long have you got left?"

"Until the end of May. I just hope I can find something else in the meantime." Karen wiped her eyes.

"Have you told Brenda?"

Karen shook her head.

"Not yet."

"Perhaps you should." Emily filled the kettle and switched it on. "First, I'm going to make you some strong sweet tea, then I'll go and find her and send her in. Stay here for as long as you need."

Karen smiled weakly. "Thank you. And you have helped, just by listening. I think I see what they mean now about a trouble shared being a trouble halved."

***

Back at the desk, Emily searched through the latest round of paperwork and was slightly surprised to find that there was no sign of any new book requests from the vicar's wife. Emily wondered if she might be deliberately keeping a low profile after being so spectacularly taken in by the April Fool prank. But when a sober-faced Brenda returned from the kitchen and she mentioned it to her, the older woman said that she'd arrived for work ten minutes early and had found Mrs Bennett waiting on the doorstep before the library opened. She'd called to renew one book and return another, and said that the vicar was taking a couple of weeks off and that they were going away on holiday.

Emily turned her attention to the trolley of recently-returned books, and noticed that *Living With Depression* had now reappeared. She hoped this was a good sign.

As she was finishing putting the books away, the library door creaked open and the Deputy Head of the primary school hobbled in on crutches. Her right leg was in plaster from the knee downwards, and five chilly-looking toes peeped out sorrowfully from a narrow slit at the base of the cast.

Emily smiled sympathetically.

"Good morning, Miss Boardman!" She nodded towards the plaster cast. "Whatever happened to you?"

By way of answer, Miss Boardman reached into her bag and extracted *A Beginner's Guide To Skydiving*.

"I don't think I'll be doing much more of that for a while,"

153

she answered ruefully, though her eyes still twinkled as she dropped the book on to the counter.

"Oh dear."

"Can you recommend something a bit more sedentary?" Miss Boardman went on.

Emily thought for a moment.

"Have you thought about tracing family history?"

Miss Boardman raised her eyebrows thoughtfully.

"I haven't, but now you come to mention it, it would be a good opportunity to have a go. Have you got anything to help me get started on it?"

"If you'd like to come this way," Emily escorted her into the reference library, "and find somewhere to sit down, I'll find you some books and bring them over. And at the moment, we've got the Births, Marriages and Deaths index lists stored here." Emily gestured towards the microfiche reader where Mr Sykes was sitting. "You can find out quite a lot from those."

"Gracious! I wouldn't know where to start," Miss Boardman sighed, as she carefully settled herself in a chair and propped her crutches up against the table.

"I'm sorry, but I couldn't help overhearing what you were just saying." Mr Sykes had appeared at their side. "Is there any way I can help?"

Emily introduced them to each other, and explained that Miss Boardman had expressed an interest in looking into family history.

"In that case, I should be honoured if you would allow me to assist you!" Mr Sykes shook her hand solemnly.

Miss Boardman returned his warm smile.

"That would be lovely, if you have the time…"

"I have as much time as you need!"

"Well, in that case, thank you very much. I think I've had quite enough excitement for the time being." Miss Boardman patted her plaster cast. "For now, I'm looking for something which will keep me out of mischief for a while!"

"Well, it will certainly keep you occupied, but there's no guarantee it will keep you out of mischief." Mr Sykes grinned, with more than just a touch of mischief of his own. "And there's no guarantee there won't be any excitement, either!"

"Really?" Miss Boardman answered. "What do you mean?"

"There's no telling what you might find, once you start looking!"

No, Emily thought, turning away quickly so that her face wouldn't betray her. There certainly isn't.

***

Returning to the desk, she was surprised to find herself face-to-face with the young man from the bank across the road. He silently handed over *How To Prepare And Present Your Own Defence Without A Solicitor*. Emily smiled, thanked him, and handed him his ticket. There was no need for her to ask him if the book had been of any use. He looked happier than she had ever seen him, and the smile on his face – a grin so wide that it was threatening to meet and tie itself in a large bow round the back of his head – told her everything she needed to know.

***

It was not until very late in the afternoon, after Mr Sykes and Miss Boardman had finally packed up their mountains of notes and gone home, that Emily was able to go back into the reference library and take a look at the microfiches herself.

"Births, 1956, June quarter…" she muttered to herself as she searched for the correct one.

Yes, there it was. *Harrison, Rosemary C. Mother's maiden surname: Brookes.*

Well, of course, Emily realised. It would be, wouldn't it? Alice and May were sisters.

She wondered what the C stood for.

Chapter Twenty-Six

Later that evening, as Carl and Emily sat by the log fire in the White Lion, Emily told Carl about her conversation with Karen. If nothing else, it served to take her mind off her own inner turmoil.

"Poor woman," Carl sighed, when she had finished.

"I know," Emily agreed. "As if she hasn't already got enough to worry about, with her husband thousands of miles away in the Falklands. I suppose I should be grateful that it isn't me they've decided to get rid of, but in a way I almost feel guilty that I'm keeping my job when she's losing hers."

Her voice trailed off and she stared into her drink. Taking a sip of Dutch courage, she drew a deep breath. There was no way she could avoid the subject any longer.

"Have you decided what you're going to do about your job?" she asked, in a very small voice.

Carl reached out and took her hand. "What would you say if I told you I'm going to take it?"

Emily stared down at the table, unable to meet his gaze.

"I don't know," she murmured.

"Why not?" he asked, equally quietly.

She looked up.

"Well, what am I supposed to say? If I sound pleased about it, then you'll think I want you to go away. If I don't, then..."

"Then what?"

"You'll think I'm being selfish and holding you back..."

She turned away. She would not let him see her cry.

But he gently tucked his free hand under her chin, and

turned her face back towards him.

"Emily, listen. I know this is probably going to sound corny, but I have to say it. I know I've only known you for a few days, but it feels as though I've known you all my life. When I'm with you, I feel that I've come home at last. And I can't begin to imagine spending the rest of my life without you. I love you, Emily. I didn't dare to hope that you might feel the same about me, but after the past few days we've had together, and especially after what you've just said... I realise I'm asking a lot of you, asking you to uproot from here and come with me, but..."

Emily gasped as she stared into those lovely blue eyes.

"You're asking me to come with you?" she answered, her voice barely above a whisper.

"Yes. And you could come on the tours, and see the world with me. How does that sound?"

"It sounds wonderful. But..."

"But what?"

"I know it sounds like a silly question, but where would I live?"

"What?" Carl looked surprised. "Where would you live? With me, of course!"

Emily hesitated. She so desperately wanted to say yes. But live with him? *Nice Girls Don't Do That...*

"What's the matter? Does it sound such a dreadful prospect?"

"No, not at all. Quite the opposite! But it's just that..."

"That what?"

Emily paused.

Yes, she had to tell him.

"Carl, do you remember I told you about Ben?"

Carl nodded. "What about him?"

"What I told you about Ben was true as far as it went, but I'm afraid I didn't tell you the whole story. The truth is, Ben dumped me because I wouldn't go to bed with him. That was the real reason why he left me; it wasn't just because he didn't want to be tied down. He evidently thought I was good enough to have sex with, but not good enough for a full, proper, committed relationship. And I found that very hurtful. And also very, very degrading."

"What a brute," Carl muttered under his breath.

"And whilst I was at university, I had a boyfriend called Tony. Or Two-Timing Tony, as I later found out. No prizes for guessing why that one ended," she sighed.

Carl took a deep breath as he tried to control his anger.

"Listen, my darling. Ben didn't leave you because you wouldn't go to bed with him. He left you because he didn't love you. Idiot that he was," he added savagely, after a moment.

Emily gasped. "What makes you say that?"

"Because if he'd really loved you, he would have cared about your feelings, too. He wouldn't have tried to bulldoze you into doing something you didn't want to do. And he certainly wouldn't have left you just because you refused." He reached up and lightly stroked her cheek. "And as for Tony, whoever he was… Well, he just didn't deserve a lovely girl like you. But I'm afraid I don't quite see where all this is leading."

"Well, nice girls aren't supposed to do that sort of thing, are they?"

"What do you mean?"

"Nice girls don't sleep with their boyfriends – dare I say it – willy-nilly, do they?" Emily tried, and failed, to suppress a giggle.

Carl grinned. "Go on."

"So, if I do agree to come with you, and live with you, will you think badly of me if I say yes?"

Carl took her hand and smiled into her eyes.

"I'll never think badly of you, my darling, whatever you decide. Quite the reverse, in fact. I think you behaved admirably with that callous brute. He definitely didn't deserve you. Come to that, I'm not sure that I deserve you. I just hope that you feel the same about me as I do about you. But I'm not asking you to come and just live with me. I'm asking you to marry me."

Emily caught her breath.

"And I'm sorry if this sounds corny," Carl went on, "but please say yes. I really, really can't live without you."

Emily gazed back into those lovely blue eyes.

"It doesn't sound corny at all," she whispered.

And, by way of answering his question, she raised her face and kissed him full on the lips. The idea that *Nice Girls Don't Do This* could not have been further from her mind.

Chapter Twenty-Seven

The next day, after a long evening spent discussing wedding plans, Emily handed in her notice to the council. She found it surprisingly easy to persuade them to keep Karen on in her place, though she was slightly frustrated at not being able to put her colleague out of her misery until the council had spoken to her directly.

It was two days later that she was suddenly called to the phone at the library.

"Emily Fisher…"

"Soon to be Emily Stone!" said an excited voice.

"Carl! What's the matter? Is everything all right?"

"Everything is fine, my darling. Listen, have you got a passport?"

"Yes. Why?"

"I've had a phone call. From Henri!"

"What?" Emily gasped. "He's still alive?"

"Very much so. And he wants to meet us. Pack a bag, my love. We're going to St-Omer."

***

"My grandfather, Nicholas, never mentioned anything about his past."

"I think I can probably explain that," Henri said quietly, as the waiter cleared away their plates.

"Oh yes?" Carl asked eagerly.

"Though I must warn you now, before I begin, that it is not

a pleasant story. Are you sure you want me to tell you?"

Carl nodded. "Yes please, if you can bear to talk about it…"

"Very well then. Before I start, may I ask: how much do you already know?"

"Very little, I'm afraid." Carl opened the folder he was carrying and extracted the piece of paper which was lying on the top of the pile. It was the list he had made of the key facts.

"What we do know," he said, glancing down at the list in his hand, "is that my grandfather was born in 1903 in Eindhoven, Holland. From looking through some of his old papers that we found after he died, we worked out that you are his brother. Your name was originally Hans, and you were born in 1900, also in Eindhoven. There was another brother, called Peter, who was born in 1902. We also found out that your parents were originally German, that they were called Wilhelm and Monika Stein, and that they married in Hamburg in 1899. And that you fought in the First World War, and so did your brother Peter, who was killed in 1918." Carl looked up at Henri. "Have we got that right?"

Henri whistled under his breath.

"Yes, that is right in every detail. And I would certainly not describe that as 'very little'! You would make a fine detective, young man!"

Carl flushed modestly.

"Thank you. But I didn't do it all on my own." He reached out and took hold of Emily's hand. "Emily translated the German letters and papers for me, and we also had a lot of help from another friend who showed us how to make sense of some of the other paperwork – birth certificates, marriage certificates, that sort of thing."

Henri nodded gravely. "Do you have those letters with you now?"

Carl nodded. "Would you like to see them?"

He carefully extracted the folder of letters and passed it across the table. The room fell silent as Henri, ashen-faced, read through the contents. Eventually, he carefully laid the papers aside and wiped away a tear.

"I'm sorry," Carl murmured. "I didn't intend to upset you."

"No, it does not matter," Henri answered. "All that was a very long time ago."

"Are you sure you want to go on with this?" Emily spoke for the first time, taking a sip of the strong dark coffee which, for her, represented the true taste of France – a taste which no café in England had ever managed to replicate.

Henri nodded.

"You have a right to know, Carl. Indeed, the world should be told the truth about what happened."

"I'm sorry, I don't quite understand."

Henri tapped the folder of papers on the table in front of him.

"I could not tell the whole truth in these letters, much as I desperately wanted to. All our letters were read by the officers before they were sent on. Anything which was deemed 'unsuitable' would have been censored."

"Yes, our friend told us about that," Carl answered quietly.

"So I could not tell our parents where we were, for example. We were told that this was to ensure that the letters would not reveal any important information to the other side, if they were to fall into the wrong hands. That I can just about understand, but we were also told that we must not write about what was happening on the front line. They told us that it was because it was classified information. But I wonder now if it was also to prevent the people at home from knowing what kind of hell we were really going through."

Henri paused.

"Go on," Carl said gently.

"That sentry, for example, the one I mentioned in the letter, told me something which made my blood run cold."

"What was that?" Emily asked nervously.

"The first night I spent on watch with him, he showed me

how a sniper could be sure of making a killing." Henri shuddered. "He said you had to watch through your field-glasses for the British soldiers on patrol striking matches to light their cigarettes. They always shared the matches, you see. Those sort of things were always in short supply, on both sides of the line. So, when you saw a match being struck – it was pitch dark, so they were always easy to spot – you knew that at least two soldiers would be using it. When you saw the first strike, you took aim, then when you saw it glow again, as they lit the second cigarette, you fired." Henri winced at the recollection. "Sometimes they even used the same match three times…"

There was no need for him to say more.

"Before you ask me," he went on after a moment, "I will tell you now that, although I spent many nights on watch duty after that, I never once did what the sniper had told me. I could never imagine killing anyone, let alone killing anyone in cold blood. We had been told that those men on the other side of the line were the enemy. But I did not see them as the enemy. Most of them were not even men. They were just innocent, frightened boys. Just like us."

"But you went over the top, didn't you?" Carl asked gently.

Henri nodded sadly.

"I had been dreading having to do that. We had all been dreading the day when the order would come. Not just because of the danger to ourselves, but also because we knew what would be expected of us once we were out there. But we also knew that anyone who refused to obey the order would be court-martialled and shot as a coward." Henri shuddered again. "My sniper friend told me that this happened to one of his friends when they first joined up, way back in 1916. Maybe that was why he behaved as he did when I first met him; he had seen what happened to those who did not toe the line."

He stared down at the table.

"So, can you tell us what happened to Peter?" Carl eventually broke the silence.

Henri nodded slowly.

"Yes, but first I will need to tell you the whole story…"

Chapter Twenty-Eight

"As you already know," Henri began, "my parents were married in Hamburg in 1899. My mother was already expecting me, so they had to marry in great haste. Immediately afterwards, they left Germany for Holland…"

"To escape the shame?" Carl asked quietly.

Henri nodded.

"Attitudes towards that sort of thing were very unforgiving at the time."

"They still are, to some extent," Emily remarked, under her breath.

"Why did they go to Holland?" Carl asked. "Could they not have gone somewhere else in Germany, for example?"

"Yes, I suppose they could have done. But there was a large electrical factory in Eindhoven. They were expanding the company and were looking for new employees, and by sheer good fortune, my father had a friend who was already working there. He had already written to my father a few months earlier, inviting him to go to Eindhoven and work with him. Going to Holland seemed to be the ideal answer to their situation. When my parents arrived in Holland, they were already married and nobody knew for how long or how short a time. So when I arrived, a few months later, there were no awkward questions."

"Ah, I see. Now it's all beginning to make sense." Carl nodded sagely.

"We had a very happy life in Holland," Henri went on. "As you know, I was born in April 1900. Peter was born in February 1902, and Nicholas – your grandfather – in December 1903."

His face grew sad. "We also had a sister, called Anna. She was born in May 1905, but she died when she was only three weeks old."

"I'm sorry to hear that." Carl reached out and gently patted the old man's hand. "What happened?"

"There was an epidemic of whooping cough in the town. We all caught it. Peter, Nicholas and I were all fortunate and recovered, but Anna..." His voice trailed off.

"We didn't find anything about her in my grandfather's papers."

Henri shook his head.

"I think our parents probably destroyed any papers relating to Anna before Nicholas ever saw them. They never talked about her afterwards – at least, not in my hearing – and Nicholas would have been too young to remember her. It is quite likely that he never even knew about her."

Emily tried, and failed, to stifle a sob. Carl reached across the table and took her hand.

"I'm sorry," she whispered in a choked voice.

Henri smiled sympathetically.

"There is no need to apologise. And please remember, what Nicholas did not know had no power to hurt him. In many ways, it was much worse for those of us who did know."

Emily looked up.

"I'm sorry," she said again. "I hadn't thought about it like that. But please go on."

"Our father worked hard at the electrical factory in Eindhoven, and a few years later he was made a manager. We were able to move to a bigger house outside the city, and we lived very comfortably for a good few years. When I was fourteen, I left school and went to work with our father in the factory. That was in April 1914..." Henri sighed. "It was only a few months later that everything changed."

"The First World War?"

Henri nodded. "Our father was detailed to go and work in a

factory which made weapons. He hated it, but he was grateful that it meant at least he did not have to go and fight. Not because he was afraid, but because he was fiercely opposed to the war and all that it represented. In many ways he was very fortunate, in that making weapons was the closest he ever came to the front line. I wish I could say the same for myself and Peter."

"What happened?"

"In the early years of the war, the army merely asked for volunteers. But by the time I was eighteen, in April 1918, they were so desperate for soldiers that they had begun conscripting all men who were eighteen or over..."

Carl nodded. "It was the same on both sides."

"...so as soon as I was eighteen," Henri went on, "even though I was living in Holland, as a German citizen, born of German parents, I was immediately called up to go and fight."

"But Peter wasn't eighteen, was he?" Carl frowned. "So how did he end up going too?"

Henri shook his head.

"Peter was just over sixteen. But he was full of youthful bravado, and as soon as he heard that I was going off to the war, he wanted to come with me. I tried to dissuade him – so did both our parents – but he would hear none of it. He came with me to the recruiting office and told the officer in charge that he was my twin brother. We were of similar height and there was a very strong family resemblance, so the officer was easily deceived. Or at least," Henri added wryly, "he was willing to be deceived."

"Didn't he ask for proof of age?" Emily asked.

Henri shook his head.

"As I said, the army was desperate for soldiers by that stage of the war. Hence, they would accept anyone who was able to fight."

"What happened next?"

"We were sent for a brief session of basic training – about

two weeks or so – then they packed us all off to the Front. I promised Mother and Father that I would try to keep an eye on Peter, but as I am sure you will understand, it was not easy once we were out there…"

Henri's voice trailed off and he stared into space. The memories were clearly agonising to recall. Emily glanced up at Carl and saw the pain and concern etched into his handsome face. She reached out and gripped his hand. Carl's eyes met hers and he managed a brief grateful smile as they waited for the old man to resume his story.

"Despite being only sixteen, Peter showed himself to be a braver soldier than many of the men who were almost twice his age. Many a time he came to the aid of others, with no thought for his own safety." Henri paused again and wiped away a tear. "And it was that selflessness which eventually proved to be his downfall."

Chapter Twenty-Nine

"Finally the day came when we were ordered over the top," Henri went on. "We were told that this was our final big push. It was supposed to end the stalemate in the trenches and finally turn the war in the Central Powers' favour."

"The Ludendorff Offensive?" Emily asked.

Henri nodded.

"It was at the beginning of August 1918. We all lined up in the trenches and waited for the signal to go over. There were too many of us to all climb the ladders and go over at the same time, so we were arranged in groups and sent over one after another. I was in the second group. As soon as the first group had gone, I could hear the gunfire and the screams from the men as they fell. There is no word to describe how terrified I felt as I waited my turn, knowing full well that those next few seconds might be my last. But I knew that if I did not go over, I would be court-martialled and shot. Rather than dying bravely on the battlefield and being remembered as a hero, I would die the ignominious death of a coward, bringing shame on my regiment and my family."

Henri shuddered involuntarily.

"Where was Peter?"

"He was in the fourth group. Or possibly the fifth; I forget exactly which. Either way, he was some way behind me. I knew that as soon as I went over, I would have no idea what happened to him, unless by some miracle we both survived..."

Carl reached across the table and laid his hand on the old man's arm.

"We know from what you wrote to your parents that Peter didn't survive," he said gently.

Henri shook his head slowly.

"So what happened? Was he killed in action?"

Henri shook his head again, but a steely look had come into his eyes, and his mouth was set in a firm hard line.

"He was killed, yes, but not in action. He was shot, by men from his own side."

"What?" Carl gasped. "Why?"

"For the reasons I have just told you. He did not go over the top."

"Why not? Did he refuse?"

Henri shook his head again.

"Perhaps I should explain at this point that when I went over the top, I had gone forward only a few paces before I was hit by a stray bullet. I do not even know which side had fired it. I fell unconscious, and knew nothing more until I woke up two days later in a military hospital, some way behind the front line. I was being tended by a young French nurse whose name was Mireille."

Henri reached across the table and took the hand of the elegant elderly lady sitting next to him.

"I was in the hospital for almost two weeks, but long before I was discharged, I knew that I loved her. When the war ended, just a few months later, we were married. We stayed in France, because I knew by then that I could never go back to Germany."

"Why was that?"

"Because of what the German army had done to my brother."

"What happened to Peter?"

Henri drew a deep breath before continuing.

"It seems that there was another man in his group who would not – or more likely could not – go over the top. When the commanding officer gave the order to advance, this man did not move. The officer screamed at him again, at which point the man completely lost his senses. He fell to the ground, screaming and twitching, as the other men scrambled up the ladders."

"But what does this have to do with Peter?"

"Peter stayed with the man and tried to calm him and encourage him. But however much he tried, it had no effect. By the time the rest of the men had gone over the top, the two of them were still left in the trench. The commanding officer did not believe that Peter had been trying to help the other soldier. He claimed that they were both trying to avoid going over. He had both of them arrested and sent for a court martial." Henri shuddered again. "They were both found guilty of cowardice, and shot at dawn the following day."

Carl winced. "Didn't they have any defence?"

Henri shook his head.

"This was not like a trial in a proper court. The officers were judge, prosecutor and jury, all in one. The men on trial could try to defend themselves when they were questioned, but under those circumstances – bearing in mind that they were, literally, on trial for their lives – they were in no fit state to even think straight, let alone try to put together a convincing defence. The guilty verdict was almost always a foregone conclusion, and the sentence was always carried out at dawn the following day. So it was with my brother. And it all happened before I had even regained consciousness after being injured," he concluded bitterly.

"How did you find out about it?" Emily asked quietly.

"The commanding officer visited me in hospital and told me about the court martial. He also told me that the General had written to our parents and informed them. I asked him if he could write and tell them that I had been injured, and that I would write to them myself as soon as I was able."

Carl nodded.

"Yes, we found that letter – and also the one which you wrote a few days later. But we didn't find the one from the

171

General."

"No, my parents destroyed it," Henri said flatly. "It was not the sort of letter which anyone would want to keep. But almost as soon as the commanding officer had left, I was then visited by another man from Peter's group; one who had survived the attack. He had been one of the last to go over the top, and had heard what was happening in the trench."

"Couldn't he have spoken up in Peter's defence?" Carl asked.

"Sadly, no. He, too, did not find out what had happened to Peter until it was too late to save him. But he wanted to be sure that I knew that my brother was no coward, and that his conviction was wholly unjust. It was then that I wrote this letter to our parents." Henri again tapped the folder on the table. "I tried to hint to them that all was not what it seemed, but once again, I could not tell them the whole truth for fear of my letter being censored."

"How did you manage to tell them?" Emily asked.

"As soon as the war was over – only a few months later – I wrote to them again and told them the same as I have just told you. I also told them that I was about to marry a French girl and that we would be staying in France. I changed my surname to Pierre. As you already know, the name Stein is the German word for stone. I chose Pierre partly because it is the French word for stone, but mainly because it is also the French equivalent of Peter. I did it out of respect for my brother, and also as a way of keeping his memory alive."

Carl nodded appreciatively.

"Why did you change your first name as well?"

"Because the name Hans is quite obviously German, and I wanted to disguise my German origins," Henri answered. "There was a lot of anti-German feeling in France immediately after the war, and I had no wish to cause distress or embarrassment to my new wife or to her family."

He hesitated, then continued. "And I am sorry if what I am about to say offends you, but that was not the only reason.

What had happened to my brother made me, frankly, ashamed to be German. From that moment onwards, I had no wish to maintain any association with a nation which had been responsible for my brother's death. Or indeed the deaths of so many other innocent young men, on both sides of the line. In one way I still felt responsible for what happened to him, because I had promised our parents that I would try to look after him." The old man's eyes filled with tears.

"The Allies weren't exactly blameless, either," Emily said gently. "In fact, I believe the British shot far more men for so-called cowardice than the Germans did. And most of them, just like your brother, were no more guilty of cowardice than you are. So please don't beat yourself up about it."

Henri looked up at her and smiled gratefully.

"Thank you. That is most comforting."

"Your family didn't stay in Holland for very long after the war," Carl remarked, after a moment's pause.

"No, they went to England. I do not know if this was just coincidence, but immediately after the war our father was moved from Eindhoven to one of the firm's new factories just outside London. It was a good opportunity for all of us to make a fresh start – me in France, them in England. Like me, our parents had no wish to remain as Germans, so as soon as they arrived in England they changed their surname to Stone."

"What happened to you when the Second World War started?" Emily asked.

Henri's mouth curled into a grin.

"By then I was fully able to pass for a patriotic Frenchman, so I did what all true patriotic Frenchmen would do under those circumstances. I joined the *Résistance*."

"Wow! That's pretty impressive!"

Henri smiled modestly.

"Not really. Mireille and I merely ran a safe house, where people were able to hide from the occupying forces. It was not impressive by the standards of the day, but all the same I was

173

proud to play my part for my adopted country. And it also did a little to ease the pain of having failed to protect my brother back in 1918. It was, perhaps, a little justice for him."

"We found a letter which you wrote to my grandfather back in 1921," Carl said. "Did he come and visit you in France?"

Henri nodded.

"Yes, Nicholas came to visit us a few times in those early years. It was during that first visit that I was finally able to tell him the truth about our brother."

"How did he take it?"

"It was a huge relief to him. He had always adored Peter, and what happened to him had been a terrible shock."

"I still can't help wondering why he never told me about him," Carl mused. "Or even about you, for that matter."

Henri sighed. "I expect that it was a painful memory which he did not wish to share; an old wound which had left a deep scar which he did not wish to disturb. He might have been afraid that if he had told you, you might start asking awkward questions..."

"It would have been a lot easier if I'd been able to ask them whilst he was still alive!" Carl said drily.

Henri chuckled. "Yes, I suppose it would. But all the same, I am glad that I have been able to answer them for you now. Is there anything else you would like to know?"

Carl considered for a moment.

"Yes, there is just one more thing. Do you know where Peter is buried?"

***

The cemetery (quite small by comparison with many of those in the area, but nonetheless smart, clean and beautifully cared-for) was situated in a quiet country lane just off the road which ran along the coast between Calais and Boulogne-sur-Mer. Carl parked the car in a layby next to the entrance, and they wandered through the gates and began to scrutinise the rows of white headstones.

"Are you sure this is right?" Carl frowned, as he peered at some of the inscriptions. "This looks like an English cemetery."

Emily consulted the map which Henri had drawn for them.

"Yes, this is definitely where he said it was. It's exactly as he describes it. Look, he even mentions the statue of Napoleon on the column over there."

Carl's gaze followed her pointing hand, to where the self-styled emperor stood gazing down majestically over the surrounding landscape.

"Well, it certainly seems to fit the bill in every other respect," he admitted. "And it is a lovely spot. If Peter is here, then I can think of far worse places for him to be. But why would he have ended up in an English cemetery?"

Emily shook her head.

"I've no idea. Though, in view of what Henri told us, I think he'd much rather Peter was buried somewhere like this than in a German military cemetery."

Carl nodded.

"Yes, I can understand that. But how do we go about trying to find him? The words 'needle' and 'haystack' spring to mind. And Henri did say it wouldn't be easy…"

Emily glanced around, then a movement in the distance caught her eye.

"Just a moment. There's a gardener over there. I'll go and ask him."

Carl watched as she trotted across to a young man who was replanting a flowerbed around the foot of the Cross of Remembrance. He couldn't hear what was being said, but he could see the young man gesture towards the far corner of the cemetery, on the opposite side to where they had come in.

Emily ran back excitedly.

"It seems that this cemetery has a few German graves, as well as all these English ones. They're in that area over there, on the far side of that path. And there aren't that many, so if Peter is here, then it shouldn't be too difficult to find him."

Carl took her hand and they made their way across the cemetery to the German plot. There were perhaps ten or fifteen rows of headstones, all tended with the same degree of care as the English ones in the rest of the cemetery. Here, at least, the fallen of both sides were treated with equal reverence and respect.

"Hmm. Not that many?" Carl frowned again. "I reckon there's probably getting on for a hundred here…"

"That's not a great deal compared with the rest of the cemetery, though, is it? Let's tackle it methodically. There's no point in us both covering the same ground, if we both know what we're looking for. So, you go over to that corner and work your way along those rows at the back; I'll start with the ones at this end."

Carl smiled. "Of course. Good thinking, Batman!"

But despite spending the next ten or fifteen minutes carefully scrutinising every headstone in the German plot, they met up again in the centre – both having failed to find any grave for a soldier called Peter Stein.

"What do we do now?" Carl scratched his head disconsolately.

Emily thought for a moment, then her face cleared.

"Come over here and look at this. I came across it whilst I was searching. I didn't think very much about it at the time, but now I'm beginning to wonder…"

She took his hand and led him back to a grave located in the second row from the end.

"Look. Did you see any like this amongst the ones you were looking at?"

The headstone, like all the others in the plot, was a simple grey stone slab with a pointed top. It bore a plain symmetrical cross, below which was engraved the words EIN UNBEKANNTER DEUTSCHER KRIEGER. Underneath that was a date: 10 August 1918.

"No, the ones I looked at all had names on. There was nothing like this. What does it mean?"

"It means 'an unknown German soldier'. And 'August' is the same in both languages. So if this really is the only one without a name, could it be Peter?"

Carl peered at the inscription again.

"Well, the date certainly fits in with what Henri told us. But I wonder why there's no name?"

Emily shook her head. "I've no idea. But, given the circumstances, maybe that's why not. Come to think of it, when people could still be hanged for murder, they were almost always buried in the prison grounds. I don't know what the procedure would have been with military executions, but perhaps they were allowed to be buried in cemeteries, provided they weren't commemorated by name. That's just an idea, though…"

Carl considered.

"Well, Henri never mentioned it, but I suppose it would certainly make sense… And it would also explain why he said it wouldn't be easy." He looked down at the headstone. "Can we assume that we've found him?"

"Without a name, we can't be a hundred per cent certain," Emily answered. "But I think ninety-nine per cent is probably close enough for most purposes, don't you?"

Carl nodded. "I wish we'd brought some flowers," he sighed.

"Just a moment. Wait here. Have a few moments on your own with your great-uncle. I'll be right back."

She gave his hand a gentle squeeze, then made her way back to where the gardener was still tending to the flowerbed. Out of the corner of his eye, Carl could see her talking to the man and pointing back towards the German plot. The young man appeared to nod his head, then bend down, pick something up, and hand it over to her. She shook his hand then walked back to where Carl was waiting.

"Here you are. It isn't much, I know, but I hope it will do for now — at least until we can come back and do this properly. I explained to that guy why we're here and what we've been doing. I know it should really be poppies, but he seemed very happy to spare us a few of these from his stock!"

"Thanks." Carl took the flowers gratefully, then crouched down in front of the headstone and laid them gently at its foot.

"Rest in peace, Peter. From your parents, your brothers, and all the family you never knew."

He straightened up and patted the top of the headstone.

"We will be back," he murmured.

***

"Was anything decided about your grandfather's headstone?" Carl asked, as they made their way back to the car.

"Yes, it's all arranged. I think my mum's planning to have a short memorial service for Granddad when it's done." She paused. "Crikey, did I just say that?"

"What?"

"My mum…"

Carl squeezed her hand. "Yes, you did. I suppose it shows that you must be getting used to the idea by now!"

Emily smiled. "I'm still trying to get my head round the fact that I've also got a brother and a sister. It's been quite a sea-change, for someone who was brought up as an only child and orphaned at seventeen!"

"How do you think your brother and sister have taken it?"

"Well, once they got over the shock, they have both been very supportive. But then, as Ruth said, it doesn't really make a great deal of difference to us. We've always got on very well. If anything, it's made us even closer than we already were."

"It's odd, isn't it?" she added after a moment. "We started out trying to find out about your family's past, but we've ended up finding out just as much, if not more, about mine."

Carl stopped walking and took her in his arms.

"Yes, it's funny how things work out. But this isn't about the past now, my love. It's about the future. Our future."

She smiled up into his eyes. Yes, the future shining out of them was looking very bright indeed.

***

"You never did tell me what your middle name was," Carl remarked later, as they were finishing their evening meal.

"Promise you won't laugh?"

"Scout's honour!" He held up three fingers in the traditional Scout salute.

"It's strange, but Emily and Rosemary were given the same middle name. It's Constance, after Gran."

"Constance? I like that. Strong and faithful."

"I hadn't thought of it like that. But I have been wondering about adding Rosemary as another middle name. What do you think?"

Carl considered. "Emily Rosemary Constance Stone? Yes, I'll drink to that!"

Emily smiled.

"I'll certainly drink to being Mrs Stone!"

They drained their glasses, and Carl rose from the table and held out his hand.

"Come along, my darling. It seems a very long time since we were on that ferry this morning. I don't know about you, but I'm certainly ready for bed."

Nice Girls Don't Do This? She happily kicked the thought into touch as she followed him up the stairs.

***

"Are you quite sure you want to?" Carl whispered, closing the bedroom door.

Emily nodded, then gave a timid smile.

"Yes, I'm sure. But I'm a little nervous. You know I've never done this before."

Carl looked at her steadily.

"Would it surprise you if I told you that I haven't, either?"

"Really?" Emily looked up in surprise.

"Really." Carl held out his arms. "And I'm glad. Very glad, my darling. Because it means that with you, it will be so much more special."

Emily melted into his waiting embrace.

"I thought it was only nice girls who were supposed to wait. I'd never thought that nice boys might want to as well."

Her lips parted as Carl's tongue found hers. Between kisses, they eagerly undressed each other and slid between the cool cotton sheets.

As with their first kiss, everything felt right; natural; how it was supposed to feel. And even a nice girl could do this, if it was shared with the love of her life…

Afterwards, she gazed at him, relishing the love and desire shining from those lovely blue eyes.

"Considering that was only our first attempt," she murmured, "it was pretty good."

"Mmm." Carl tightened his arms around her, unwilling to withdraw from her. "But I think we still need to practise a lot more. And we've got the whole night ahead of us…"

Chapter Thirty

Emily and Carl had set the date of their wedding for the middle of July, and she had arranged to carry on working at the library until the middle of June. At the time it had felt as though it was months (rather than weeks) away, but her final day came round all too quickly.

She had been expecting it to be a day just like any other, but Brenda and Karen – her husband now safely on his way home from the South Atlantic – had clearly had other ideas. Emily arrived at work to find a huge banner, bearing the legend 'GOOD LUCK EMILY AND CARL' strung above the library door. Trays of drinks, nibbles and sandwiches were on offer all day for the library customers, including – Emily couldn't help noticing – quite a few people who had never darkened the library's door until that very morning. Oh well, she thought, if it brings us – sorry, them – a few more customers, then that can only be a good thing.

Amongst the guests who stayed for most of the day were Mr Sykes and Miss Boardman, who was now out of plaster and managing to walk with just a stick.

"I have a request, fair lady," Mr Sykes said to Emily, after his umpteenth cup of tea.

"Oh yes?"

"I know you're going to be busy on the seventeenth of July, but please can you keep the third free?"

"I should think so. Why do you ask?"

By way of answer, he handed Emily an expensive-looking envelope and watched as she opened it.

Mr Norman Alfred Sykes and Miss Elizabeth Mary Boardman request the pleasure of your company on the occasion of their marriage…

Emily squealed with delight. "Congratulations, both of you! I hope you'll be very happy."

"And no presents, please. Just the pleasure of your company. Be there or be square."

"Of course we'll be there," said a familiar voice behind her. "After all, you're coming to ours, aren't you?"

Emily turned. Carl was holding a large white cardboard box, which he opened to reveal an exotic, dark brown cake, decorated with swirls of cream and black cherries.

"Where on earth did you get that?"

"I ordered it from the café across the road. It's one of their new specialities."

"What is it?" Karen asked, intrigued.

"Black Forest Gâteau. They say it's an authentic taste of Bavaria."

"And is it?"

"I've no idea. I haven't tried eating any of Bavaria. I expect it tastes rather earthy. But the cake looks very nice."

Emily grinned, then picked up a knife and began cutting the massive confection into slices.

"Excuse me?"

Emily looked up. Standing in front of the desk was an elegant middle-aged lady. She had short fair hair, stylishly cut and tastefully highlighted, and her skin was lightly suntanned. She looked vaguely familiar, though it was a few moments before Emily twigged who she was.

"Mrs Bennett! How lovely to see you. Did you enjoy your holiday?"

The vicar's wife nodded and smiled.

"Yes, thank you. It was just what we needed. I'd forgotten just how long it's been since we last had a proper holiday. I've brought these back."

She reached into her shopping bag and pulled out *Coping With Comfort Eating* and *How To Lose Seven Pounds In Seven Days*.

"To be honest, I'd completely forgotten I'd borrowed them." She smiled sheepishly. "I expect they're rather overdue by now. How much do I owe?"

Emily smiled. "I think I can probably waive the fines just this once. Would you like a little refreshment?" She offered her a piece of the Black Forest Gâteau and Mrs Bennett's face lit up.

"Thank you. I shouldn't really, but since you've been so kind as to offer, it would be churlish of me to say no, wouldn't it?"

For the next few minutes she munched away at a piece of the dark sticky cake, clearly relishing every sinful mouthful.

"Thank you. That was delicious," she said, carefully wiping a smear of cream from her chin with a tissue.

"Oh, there is just one more thing." She turned back to Emily with a mischievous gleam in her eyes, then lowered her voice to a whisper.

"I believe there's a book called *How To Enjoy Great Sex After The Menopause*. Do you have a copy, by any chance?"

***

"You had that book in your hand when I first met you," Carl murmured into Emily's ear, as Mrs Bennett tucked the book into her bag and made her way to the door.

There had been a time, not so very long ago, when Emily would have blushed crimson at the memory. But now, she merely turned to the love of her life and grinned.

"I know. Not very romantic, was it?"

"Who knows?" Carl raised his eyebrows thoughtfully. "That book might be the most romantic thing to hit the vicarage for a long time!"

Emily considered.

"Well, at any rate, it's a rather more promising offering than *The Garbage Gourmet!*"

"Talking of food, Miss Fisher," Carl declared solemnly, picking up a piece of the gâteau, "how do you fancy a German bite?"

Emily chuckled. Life with Carl, wherever in the world they might find themselves, was certainly never going to be dull.

"Marks out of ten?" she asked, as he took his first mouthful.

Carl chewed thoughtfully before answering. "Nine-and-a-half, I think."

Emily sighed in mock exasperation.

"Does anything *ever* get ten?"

Carl put down the plate and took her in his arms.

"Only you, my darling. Only you."

THE END

Fantastic Books
Great Authors

Meet our authors and discover our exciting range:

- Gripping Thrillers
- Cosy Mysteries
- Romantic Chick-Lit
- Fascinating Historicals
- Exciting Fantasy
- Young Adult and Children's Adventures

Visit us at:
www.crookedcatbooks.com

Join us on facebook:
www.facebook.com/crookedcatpublishing

Lightning Source UK Ltd.
Milton Keynes UK
UKOW05f2302130714

235071UK00001B/1/P